MERCURY'S FLIGHT

THE STORY OF A
LIPIZZANER STALLION

Annie Wedekind

Feiwel and Friends • New York

A Feiwel and Friends Book
An Imprint of Macmillan

Library of Congress Cataloging-in-Publication Data Available

ISBN: 978-0-312-38427-2

Book design by Barbara Grzeslo

Feiwel and Friends logo designed by Filomena Tuosto

First Edition: 2011

10 9 8 7 6 5 4 3 2 1

mackids.com

Dear Reader,

Welcome to the Breyer Horse Collection book series!

When I was a young girl, I was not able to have a horse of my own. So, while I dreamed of having my own horse one day, I read every book about horses that I could find, filled my room with Breyer model horses, and took riding lessons.

Today, I'm lucky enough to work at Breyer, a company that is known for making authentic and realistic portrait models of horse heroes, great champions, and of course, horses in literature. This beautiful fiction series is near to my heart because it is about horses whose memorable stories will take their place alongside the horse books that I loved as a child.

This series celebrates popular horse breeds that everyone loves. In each book, you'll get to appreciate the unique characteristics of a different breed, understand their history, and experience their life through their eyes. I believe that you'll love these books as much as I do, and that the horse heroes you meet in them will be your friends for life.

Enjoy them all!

Stephanie Mazyo

Stephanie Macejko
Breyer Animal Creations

CHAPTER 1

MY WAR STARTED, I SUPPOSE, IN THE SPRING of 1939. Of course, I did not know this at the time. I did not know that life was going to change—I was about to say *forever*, but the strange thing is, that isn't true. Life did not change forever. And that gave hope to people—that some things continued, after the bombs and the tanks and the guns. Even if we were only horses.

Only horses. I can imagine what the Colonel would think of that idea. For the Colonel, the white horses of Lipizza were everything—his life, his work, his mission. Of course in the beginning, in my beginning, I did not know that such a man as the Colonel existed. His rather horselike face, with its long crooked nose, expressive eyebrows, and creases that ran in grooves down his thin cheeks, had not yet peered over my stall, a look of dismay on his face, shouting, *God, Max, do something to cheer him up!* It was one of the moments at *Die Spanische Reitschule*—or the Spanish Riding School—that I never

1

forgot, even when home was so far away that I feared I would forget the way it smelled.

In the beginning, in my beginning and in most everyone else's, was a mother. A mother and a place that shaped my character with equal importance. Meadowlands starred with flowers, mountain streams, apple trees, and the air as cool and fresh as the sparkling, dancing waters that fed our pasture . . . a heaven of horses. But if you come from such a place, how can you bear to leave? How can you bear to grow up?

It was different for me, this heaven. I experienced its beauty much as the other colts and fillies did, grazing the summer pastures, running and frisking and experimenting with our strong, young bodies. We were dark moons orbiting the white suns of our mothers, and this is where I was unlike my companions, growing up in a world next to but not the same as theirs. For my sun, my mother, was unlike the others. She did not want her dark moon. She did not want me.

My earliest memories of Mercurio, the beautiful white mare who foaled me, are indistinct, both because it was so long ago and because I did not have the cause or the urge to revisit them, until my advanced training began. I suppose the first thing I knew, and now the first thing

I remember, is not her, but her absence. Among my first memories is being alone, dirty and unable to stand, in a large, dark stall, sweet smelling with hay and that clean barn dust. It was comfortable but empty, and what I wanted at that moment was to be near something, near someone, brought close and warmed. But there was nothing but the deep evening, the quiet sounds of unseen horses rustling in the adjoining stalls, the song of summer outside the doors I could not see over. I felt, unaccountably, that I had done something wrong. And though the night was mild, I was so cold.

How does a new creature, who knows almost nothing, know that something is missing? I suppose because we ache for it–for the rough, cleansing tongue, the throaty nicker of concern, the muzzle gently pushing us to our feet and toward the large, warm body and the milk it gives. Somehow, we know we need a mother, and when she does not come . . . well, I was going to say that we– that *I*–assumed it was my fault, but that feeling came later. First, the world was simply centered around a great, dark hole: my need and her absence.

It was hands–human hands–that cleaned me, warmed me, and fed me. I remember little except for the strange smells that accompanied them, how I first distrusted them and their alien scent, and then learned that these thin, upright figures with their baffling hands and their near-constant stream of foreign speech were to be my caretakers. I had yet to meet another horse. As far as I knew, I was the only one in the universe. Doesn't every paradise contain its dark side?

. . .

MY NAME IS FAVORY MERCURIO. IT WAS THE only one I could have, following the dictates of traditional Lipizzaner stallion nomenclature. I suppose if I had been born in another place, and my flanks did not bear the crest of Piber, I could have been Smoky or Peanut or Lucky. But I am Favory Mercurio, literally the compound of my father, Favory Toscana, and my erstwhile mother, Mercurio. I have grown into my name now, but in the beginning the people must have thought it was too big for me, for they gave me another: Pipl. It was my first caretaker, Jan, himself a very young man, who christened me. Jan fed me, groomed me, and kept me alive in the weeks before I found my surrogate mother. It seemed he was always there when I woke from my uneasy, lonely sleep, and now I see that he must have been worried indeed to spend so much time on me. The Piber nursery is a very busy place, and the grooms

5

do not have time for babysitting. Still, there was Jan's face, round and smiling, and his soft, measured voice, saying, "Pipl, my little *chlápek*,* you must eat more, you must drink more. . . ."

I think I was in a sort of borderland, those first weeks. I had not fully decided to live. The world was incomprehensible and I was alone, except for Jan, and the doctor, and the other men who cleaned my stall and prodded my flanks. Why live? I existed in twilight, barely eating, barely drinking, sleeping and dreaming of I don't know what. Jan said to the doctor, "He won't take hold. He's slipping away from us." And that was exactly right.

And then one evening at dusk I was taken out of my stall for the second time. Jan tied a soft cloth about my neck and led me through the door, his arm cradled around my shoulders. I stumbled. I had not been able to walk much yet. But Jan helped me up and said encouraging things and kept moving me forward, down the corridor of the barn, toward a covered arena. Now I could see the heads of other horses in the stalls and I felt—something. Something that had been

* Czech for "fellow"

asleep quickened in me. I walked on, sniffing the air and trembling.

There, standing in the arena, tied to a post, was a sturdy white mare. As I moved unsteadily forward, I could smell her hay-sweet breath, and something else—something warm and compelling, a smell I would later think of as my first idea of *home.* What does home mean to a horse? It means where you belong, and if you know anything about herd animals, no matter how fancily tricked up in saddles and brands and braids, no matter how individually gifted, all we really want is to know where we belong. Whether a herd, a barn, a team, or, now, a mother—we need a place in this world. And as I caught the scent of the mare, looking at me with calm interest, I let loose my first sound on earth, a plaintive sort of bleat, I'm sure, but it was a cry I could no longer contain. *Mama!*

She was not, of course, my mother. She was Galanta, fourteen years old, a respectable broodmare who had recently foaled. She was known for her forgiving temperament and for raising healthy colts and fillies. This was an experiment to see if she would consent to adopt me. I did not know any of this as I rushed toward her, nor did I have any idea what to do once I reached her side. But Galanta knew, and after an earnest sniffing and vigorous nudging that almost toppled me, she expertly guided my muzzle toward her belly and her milk. It was, simply, bliss. The men laughed with relief as my little bush of a tail waved madly and I grunted with happiness. For the first time, I felt like I knew what I was—a horse—and what I was supposed to do.

. . .

I HAD TO SHARE GALANTA WITH HER NATURAL son, Neapolitano Galanta (otherwise known as Ned), who had been born eight weeks before me. Ned—stocky, splendidly formed, well-fed, and supremely confident— was unfazed by his sudden acquisition of a stepbrother.

"Well," he told me when we first met, "my mother's the best." As if to say it would be a pity to limit Galanta's maternal talents to merely one foal. Ned was kind to me, if a bit condescending, because he was happy and cared for, and our early years together were my first tutorial on this essential fact: How a horse acts toward others (horses, men) is often a direct reflection of how he feels about himself. It is not the self-satisfied horse that kicks or balks or bolts. It is the frightened horse, the insecure horse . . . the horse that could have been me had I not had Galanta, Ned, and then my great teachers.

In retrospect, having since sired foals of my own, Galanta put up surprisingly little fuss about taking on an orphaned stranger. But that was her personality—a kind of insistent competence and matter-of-factness about the world. All she told me was, "I suppose I should have let you die? Not likely, Pipl. I knew you were a fighter. But you needed a chance." She never seemed anxious about me, or about Ned for that matter. She took it for granted that she would raise fine, strong foals, and the most she tried to impart to us, beside food and warmth and certain nuzzles when we had done something stupid and were embarrassed, was common sense. She was an aristocrat.

And it was an aristocratic setting. From the low-slung, orderly buildings with their creamy walls and ochre roofs to the magnificent Austrian landscape, lush, sloping meadows lined with upright cypresses and fringed with apple orchards, the entire Piber stud farm seemed to breathe the air of centuries, to exist outside of time. This land had seen the breeding of horses since the eighteenth century, and from empire to empire, it endured. Even early on, we colts and fillies were impressed with our fortune and the expectations it carried: *This is for you*, our home seemed to say. *Don't waste it.*

The other horses and men gave us much the same message, in their different ways. There were rules to be followed as well as freedom to be enjoyed. After an initial, comforting confinement with Galanta and Ned, our rather unusual triumvirate was blended with the rest of the mares and foals, in a large pasture. Here we met the other colts and fillies born in our year, but I was shy then and remember mostly sticking by Ned.

Ned has always been worth sticking by. Two months my senior, he seemed older in other ways as well, or at least more impressive. I will always see him as my big brother. Black where I was brown, compact and well-muscled where I was leggy and weedy, we were as un-alike as two colts could be. Here is Ned:

"Want to go look over there? Think I see a butterfly. A big one."

Pipl: "Way over there?"

Ned: "Sure. Stay right by me. We'll scare that old butterfly. Chase him!"

Pipl: "Seems sort of far . . . I don't see a butterfly."

Ned: "I'll bring you right to him. You'll touch your nose right on his wings! Stay by me. . . ."

And so I did. I would stay by Ned, and indeed he'd bring me to the butterfly, and I would touch its fluttering yellow wings with my muzzle, and Ned would caper after it, running surefootedly among the dips and swoops of the hills. He was always bringing me along. Until . . .

"Boys!"

Galanta's neigh would ring over the fields and we would scamper home—eagerly, in my case, and reluctantly, in Ned's.

"Aw, Mother! I almost caught that one, too!"

"With what, Ned? Your tail? Scootch, Pipl. Make room for your brother."

And Galanta's two dark moons would rest, side by side, in the late afternoon sunshine.

. . .

ALTHOUGH MUCH WAS EXPECTED OF US, OUR introduction to our world was always gentle. The men of Piber were calm, reliable people whose attitude mirrored Galanta's. They believed in us, and unless we gave them reason to think otherwise, they assumed our good intentions and abilities. I will never forget the day we were finally separated from our mothers, when we were about six months old. Of course, I felt heartbroken and confused as we were led to a barn away from our dams, a pack of jostling, uncoordinated, desperate children crying out for the mares. The first night was especially difficult for me. My feelings of abandonment were acute—it was as if I were experiencing my mother's rejection all over again. Galanta's sudden, inexplicable absence seemed to call up buried memories: the flash of teeth, the furious shove, hands pulling me away . . . away from the mare who should want me. Shouldn't she? It was a terrible night. I shivered next to Ned, who wasn't much better off. But in the morning, there was Jan, as unflappable and sturdy as always, stroking our manes and speaking in his gentle drone:

"Now then, my boys, let's have breakfast and a trot outside, and things won't seem so bad, eh? It's still the same old world—you're just getting bigger." And when I refused to follow Ned out the door, Jan seemed mildly surprised and regretful, as if he expected more from me, but oh well. It took me two hours to get my courage up to join the new herd of foals, now chasing one another in the golden autumn fields, and when I did, Jan was quietly satisfied.

"Knew you'd get there in the end, young man," he told me confidently. "I expected no less."

And I did always get there in the end, though by my own, slower route. It was my nature to approach new things hesitantly, and though I was still contemplating the bridle when Ned was already trotting in fluid circles from a longe line; though I stood and stared for many hours at the older colts (whose herd we joined when we were two) while my companions were eagerly joining them in mock battles and races, I did get there. And in the process, I earned a new nickname from a Viennese man observing our training: *Schnecki.**

Piber was the proper place for taking one's time. The days passed with their own rhythm, and the seasons gave a cadence to our routines . . . summer in the alpine mountains, running with Ned and the other stallions, winter in the Hof Wilhelm, outside the main stud, and snow days spent in group exercise in an outdoor arena. Visitors came and watched us at our work and play, men from Vienna, a place often spoken of, but never explained, itself like a dream. But there was a horizon to this gentle world—a destination that I dimly glimpsed as I learned and played and stared out toward the mountains, thinking of nothing in particular except life and grass and Ned and whether I would ever fully understand what the men wanted from us and whether it even really mattered. Perhaps this was all there was. The green world of our province, Styria, made for us. But of course, it wasn't the end. It was only the very beginning.

---

* Wienerisch (the German dialect spoken in Vienna, Austria) for "slow-poke," or "little snail"

CHAPTER 2

NED WAS THE FIRST TO POINT OUT TO ME that our class—the horses born in Spring 1933— were now the oldest stallions in our herd. Of course, I'd noticed the departure of our big brothers—most of whom I'd avoided as much as possible, letting Ned run interference when the jostling and nipping and kicking of the near-daily social jockeying got the best of me, as it usually did. Since I bowed out of any attempt at herd dominance, happily mooning along by myself or with Ned or another low-ranked colt, I could hardly start throwing my weight around when new youngsters joined our herd. Nor did I care to. I left the new colts alone, unless they wanted to join me on a walk or a fly swish. But I never had any interest in leading or fighting. I liked to watch the men: Though familiar, they were a puzzle. I watched them with other horses; I watched them as they handled me. I thought about their voices, low and full of praise, matter-of-fact and lightly tinged with disapproval.

I watched in astonishment as they rode their own horses—tall, thin bays and chestnuts that stood out from our gray-white-and-brown-mottled bunch like migrating birds visiting from another land. I thought about Galanta, whom I missed. I sometimes caught sight of her being led from the barn to the mares' field. Sometimes she met my eye and gave me a brief whinny, but mostly she kindly ignored me, full of the fresh life growing inside her. I don't think Ned thought of her at all.

Instead, Ned was full of plans for the future, a future that had been far from my mind.

"You know the men from Vienna are coming soon," he told me matter-of-factly. "They're coming to see us, just like they did with the others who have left."

"Where did they go?" I wondered, late as always to grasp the big picture.

Ned stared at me with gentle astonishment. "To *Die Spanische*. Don't you know anything?"

Well, no. I didn't.

"They judge us," he continued. "They take the best horses to the school, and sell the rest. Last year, Maestoso Fortuna was sent up, and our brother Conversano Galanta, and . . ."

I stopped listening. *They judge us.* I suddenly felt very

cold, stunned like a bird who has fallen into a drift of snow. *They judge us.* I had been judged once and found wanting. If my own mother wouldn't keep me, why would the men from Vienna? What were we being judged *for*? And again, the great question echoed in my mind: *What is our purpose with men?*

"What are they looking for?" I managed to ask.

Ned snorted. "The best, obviously. You know, the horses that are the best. But don't worry—you and I are *definitely* going up." He nonchalantly bent his head to graze.

It occurred to me that Ned had no more idea of what the men wanted than I did, but what he had was total confidence that whatever it was, he had it, and in spades. That his confidence extended to me was comforting, though I think Ned sometimes forgot that we were not actually brothers. It was nice of him—but I never forgot. It was obvious to me that I was different. That I was missing pieces, or that my pieces looked a little different from the other horses'. Ned was whole, and I was still putting myself together. More than any of the other colts, I looked to the men to help me understand the world and my place in it. What would happen if they, like my mother, did not want me anymore?

NED TOLD ME NOT TO WORRY ABOUT THE inspection, and he set a very good example. But I couldn't help it. I was suddenly aware of the impermanence of my world—not because the stately confines of Piber would change, but because *I* would be put to a test. I would pass or I would fail, without, perhaps, ever knowing why. *Die Spanische* itself I didn't bother with. While I could endlessly contemplate the view from my favorite summer meadow, I did not spare much thought for the unknown. At the moment, I knew that Piber and the school were linked, were a sort of field that I would continue to graze if I was deemed worthy. I wanted to belong to this continuum, even in Vienna, or wherever. I knew that these things must be bound up in *who we were*, why we were here, and the continuing mystery of what the men intended. To be cut off from the other Lipizzaners, and from the men who cared for us and taught us, seemed unbearable. I was a part of something. I did not want to be cast off.

So, senior in our herd of young stallions, Ned and I luxuriated in the summer mountain fields. But I felt like I always had one ear cocked toward autumn—and change. We *were* changing. My stubborn dark coat aside, I could feel other, deeper changes in my body. My legs, trotting and bouncing me along the rock-strewn slopes, were stronger, and my stride somehow springier. I took great delight in my legs and liked to trot up and down my favorite meadow, jumping rocks and the narrow, trickling streams that ran in ribbons down the hillsides. *One two three four* . . . jog to Ned and touch noses . . . *One two three four* . . . over to the yellow flowers and up, up to the sweet grass . . . *one two three four . . . bounce! Over the stream and bounce! Another jump for the fun of it . . . hop!* Ned always tried to get me to chase him, to race like the other colts. There was nothing he loved more than running flat out, full speed, in a high-spirited game of tag. But I wasn't very fast, despite my longish legs, and the colts played too rough for me. When Ned and the others wanted to tussle, I retired to the shade to graze and to contemplate the blue Styrian skies, wondering what changes the change of season would bring.

· · ·

WHEN THE MOUNTAIN AIR COOLED AND THE leaves began to change colors, the herds were collected from the summer fields and brought back to the warmth and structure of the barns, the frequent handling of men, and the routines we had learned to expect with the change of weather. It was a bit difficult for me. I've never liked change—most horses don't—but I in particular, with my slower nature, was grumpy until, after a few days, I grew philosophical.

Of course, the benefit of the barns was that I could resume my study of our handlers, whom we saw in the summer, but not with the frequency and intimacy that our fall and winter quarters provided. I greeted Jan with enthusiasm, and the doctor and stable boys who cleaned our stalls. I was thoroughly and luxuriously groomed and led about and petted and exercised in hand. My legs were admired, and that gave me a great deal of pleasure. We still got to socialize in the covered arena, and I complacently trotted around Ned and the quieter colts while the noisy ones resumed their summer antics, some lower-ranked horses hoping that the change in locale might bring a change in their herd position. I still saw no benefit in the constant jockeying and maneuvering. I took whatever friends came my way and ignored the rest. I was never lonely, and I was never punished for cheek. No horses seemed to actively dislike me, and they all had been schooled early on by Ned to leave me alone when I wanted it. I was different, but I was still a member of the family.

There was a bustle one morning in the courtyard

outside the stables, the growling of cars and then the slamming of doors and men's voices calling out to one another. I poked my head out of my stall to see what was happening. A group of strange men were standing in the driveway, talking with Jan and our other handlers. I watched them curiously, taking especial note of a well-built, solemn-faced person with a quiet way of standing, a little separate from the group. He had a pleasant voice, and I enjoyed watching his movements. After a few minutes of conversation, I realized that though his face was stern, his eyes held warmth. As the men approached the barn, he took a position in the back of the group, much as I might have done.

I swear that it didn't occur to me until the visitors had made their way halfway down the aisle of the barn, leading out some horses, patting others, passing by some stalls with no comment, that the day of the dreaded inspection had arrived. That this was it. It had been such an absolutely ordinary morning, and with my sensitivity to Jan and the others I thought I would have noticed any tension or excitement they were feeling. Of course, what I couldn't know was that the decision, for all intents and purposes, had already been made. Or was being made during every day of the three and a half years I'd been alive.

So far, two horses had been led to a paddock outside, one of whom was Ned. Obviously, the paddock was the place to be. I briefly considered whinnying to Ned, but decided to keep quiet. It couldn't be wise to raise an unseemly ruckus with the visitors so close to my stall. And finally, the soft tapping of the heels of their boots grew nearer, their voices swelled, then quieted, and four faces, wearing varying expressions, were peering in the window of my stall.

I stood very still, ears forward, head cocked so I could see them clearly. Jan's dear face had a hint of a smile; the stable boy who accompanied them smelled of nerves. One of the visitors, the man obviously in authority, looked cross. And the one I thought I liked—perhaps recognized?—remained in the background, with a thoughtful air about him.

"He hasn't gotten any better looking, has he?" the leader grumbled.

"I suppose I'm used to him, so he looks as he should to me," was Jan's mild reply.

"He's as brown as the day he was born."

"He does everything in his own time, Herr Director. In fact—" But the man in charge, the "Director," cut him off.

"Well, let's see him, anyway."

My relief was so strong, but collided so sharply with the surprise of hearing that I wasn't good looking, that it took me a moment to gather my wits. The Director snorted as Jan encouraged me forward, and, rather dazed, I stepped gingerly out from my stall.

"Come, Schnecki, come, old fellow." At least I had Jan's comforting figure beside me as we walked out into the soft, gray October morning.

I was handed over to a groom and led into the paddock, where Ned and two other stallions were being walked. I was too far from Ned for conversation, so I did my best to steady myself, breathing in the autumn air and catching hints of the men with it. The visitors had been joined by the manager of the stud, a man I knew well from his frequent visits to our fields and barns. I was now almost positive that the quiet visitor had been here before, too, perhaps had watched us playing in the summer meadow. . . . No matter. Though I still did not know the nature of the test that faced us, I knew I was being asked to walk, so walk I would. I focused on the beats of my hoofs and the steady stride of the groom beside me. *Just walk*, I told myself. *That's all for now.*

We walked and trotted and stood, then walked and

trotted in the other direction. We walked in circles, backed a few steps. We trotted across the diagonal. I tried to pay strict attention to the groom beside me, to sense his will above and beyond his obvious directions. That was always my strategy when working with men: to try to understand the motivation behind the command. I doubted I would ever grasp their *reasons*—they were too alien. But I could try to interpret the desires that lay under the chirrup, the pressure of the nose band, the energy emanating from my two-legged guide. The groom, whom I liked, was easy to read. *Brisk. Energy, now. Collect. Listen close. Straight, go straight. Stretch out. Match my rhythm. Steady.*

Easy, and a good way to stay in the moment, when there was so much going on around me. The Director lit a cigar, Jan cleared his throat, and the quiet man was talking to our manager, too softly for me to hear. A handful of birds flew in a noisy gust from a nearby tree. The church bell rang. A filly was being led from the far barn to the field, and the third horse in the ring—a very prepossessing stallion named Pluto Adrina—catcalled to her, drops flying from his nostrils as he neighed and snickered at her. His groom tugged his lead shank, averting a charge. Ned laughed.

Finally our grooms led us back to the center of the paddock and halted us in a line, facing our judges. At least I assumed that's who they were. To my mind, we hadn't done a great deal worthy of judgment, but men were mysterious. Who knew what they saw when they looked at us, eyes narrowed over cigar smoke, or open and gray and curious, or twinkling nicely like Jan's? Apparently they thought I was ugly. That was something I would have to mull over, back in the barn with Ned.

"Not a big group this year, Alois," the Director remarked.

"Well, no-o," Dr. Besel, the head of Piber, murmured, "but talented, I think."

"I'm not convinced by the last one. What do you call him? Schnecki? We must measure him. He looks too big for the quadrille."

"He's fifteen point two, exactly," Jan said.

"Better hope he's done growing. That head won't win any beauty prizes. Awkward, altogether awkward."

"You must hear me—one moment, please!" Jan's cry startled me and I threw my head up. He sounded quite pained.

"I think we *have* heard you," said the Director. "And

I'm still not impressed with the quality of *all* of this year's candidates."

"Pardon me." This from the quiet visitor, leaning forward toward Jan. "I would like to hear your comments, please."

Poor Jan was a bit pink and flustered, but his voice steadied as he addressed the others. "Granted, Schnecki is a bit odd looking *now*, but his legs, and especially his hindquarters, are strong and well-formed—I see no true fault in his conformation. He's just a colt, after all, and has much growing to do. But it is his personality that is unique, his mind and his understanding—"

"He was an orphan, correct? His dam rejected him?" The Director's words made me cold inside. This was awful. I stared down at the ground, hoping it would all be over soon.

"It was most inexplicable," our manager said. "But he did well with his foster mother, Galanta. She's a wise mare. That's her natural son, Neapolitano Galanta, on the left. A better-than-fine colt, I believe."

"Yes, that one is obviously suitable. But his foster brother . . ."

"His foster brother is one of the most intelligent horses I've worked with," Jan returned. "He's not quick, but once he understands a thing, it's his forever. You never have to teach him twice. And his role in the herd—well, it's remarkable. He is absolutely respected by the others, though he has never fought for rank. I am confident he will work extremely well in close proximity with other horses. Not only that, but he is the finest jumper of the lot—he enjoys it and it comes naturally to him. But really—you have to understand me—it's his willingness to learn that most impresses me. His attention is positively uncanny."

"And his spirit?" asked the quiet man. "He seems subdued to me."

"His spirit is a quiet one," Jan acknowledged, "and he's very sensitive. He can get a bit low, I suppose."

"Then we'll have to keep him cheerful," the man said lightly. "Come, Herr Graf. Let's give him his chance. An intelligent horse is always welcome at *Die Spanische*, yes?"

And with that one easygoing remark, my new friend secured my place. Everyone relaxed, shook hands, and the visitors made their way back to the automobile. We were led back to our stalls and given our feed, just like any other day. Any other day that changed the course of your life entirely.

CHAPTER 3

*C*LICKETY CLACK, CLICKETY CLACK, CLICK-*ety clack.*

The sound of the train filled my ears and my very dreams as we sped north, north to Vienna, north to the future. . . .

Clickety clack clickety clack.

I stuck my nose out the window Jan had opened for me, breathing in the cold, delicious scent of melting snow as well as the harsh soot-smell of this great black horse we rode. I found the train very conducive to thinking and was surprised how much I liked the sensation of motion. We were comfortably housed in large boxcars cushioned with fresh straw, and Jan slept with me at night. It was a cozy way to leave one home for another, and as I leaned out to survey the splendid countryside and the great chasing clouds scouring the sky, I felt hopeful, even eager, for what lay ahead.

That spring, just starting, was particularly lovely. At Piber, our herd was full of spirits, and the air was heady with rising sap and leaf bud, soil relaxing from its frost and fast-rushing streams spilling over their banks. We were often muddy, often wet, almost always happy. And underneath the dirt and water, our coats were changing, lightening toward the freckled white of our mothers and fathers. Well, all except mine. I suppose it should come as no surprise that I was taking longer than the others to shed my dark cloak. I was still absolutely, solidly brown, and Ned teased that if he didn't know better, he'd say I was the son of a draft horse.

I've said before that I let Ned do the thinking about what lay ahead, but at the moment, Ned was in a forward car, quite out of hearing, so I let the wind breeze through my mane and considered, for myself, all that Vienna might mean for us.

The great city formed part of my thoughts. Another part was occupied with chewing over Jan's words. I suppose what surprised me most was his assessment of my status in the herd. *Did* all the other stallions respect me so? That would be funny, considering that I never fought to earn their respect. I always thought it was Ned who secured my position as an independent horse. It was all rather confusing. But I liked that Jan mentioned my jumping. I hoped I'd have more streams to cross, more logs to leap, once we reached *Die Spanische*.

But as our journey continued and I watched the thickly wooded hills and neat farms give way to unfamiliar structures, closely packed and laced with roads, I began to wonder what sort of land Vienna was, exactly. Since I knew only Piber, I pictured the capital as another stud farm, on a grander scale. I knew there would be more men, more stallions, and different routines, but I didn't know that the very earth would be transformed to something made by man. As the clusters of buildings grew ever denser, the train slowed and finally came to a noisy stop in a sort of yard with a bewilderment of tracks, sheds, and men moving over the barren landscape. I ventured to call to Ned and was reassured to hear his eager neigh in return.

We're here!

. . .

IT WAS GOOD THAT I'D HAD SO MANY QUIET hours on the train for contemplation, for as soon as I set hoof on the rail yard of the Südbahnhof, things seemed to happen very quickly. The sheer number of men—and their vehicles—was breathtaking. The moment I turned my head in response to one horn, shout, or whistle, another sound would catch my attention. Anchoring me to the bustling scene were Jan, calmly running his hands down my legs and affixing my lead rope, and Ned, prancing at his groom's side, eyes bright with excitement. Next to them, my abbreviated herd, I felt quite ready for anything.

Except, perhaps, to say good-bye. If I hadn't been so distracted by the clang and din of the world around me, I might have been more prepared for the moment when Jan handed my lead rope over to a dark-haired groom, neat in a gray uniform and cap, and gave my neck a final caress. Startled, I pulled back from the stranger and looked in distress to Jan. But he only smiled and said calmly, "Off you go, Schnecki, old man. You're going to your proper home. Don't disappoint us." Then, in a sharper tone to the groom: "Don't force him. Let him understand you and have time to think."

"Yes, sir," said the stranger who now had his hand on my halter. His fingers smelled sweet, and I soon discovered why as he dipped down into his pocket and retrieved a lump of sugar.

"There's a good fellow," the groom—hardly more than a boy—told me as I lipped the treat from his rough palm. "What is it you call him again?"

"Schnecki. He might seem a bit thick at first, but he's the thinkingest horse I ever raised." Jan laughed, then took my face between his hands and gave me a kiss on both cheeks. The groom smiled, and whispered in my ear, "We'll get along well, Schnecki. I have a feeling." And with that, he shook hands with Jan and turned me away. That was my last impression of my friend, his kiss and his laughter, which warmed me as it was so rare. If Jan was confident, so should I be.

Our procession began on the slushy streets of the city. Pluto Adrina led the way, then Ned, then me. I was almost as interested in the young man beside me as I was in the absorbing, hectic street scene through which we walked, and he soon united my interests by narrating our progress through the city.

"We have a thirty-minute-or-so walk ahead of us, old man," he began. "Perhaps less, but we must go carefully in all this slop. The snow must be much nicer in Styria, eh? Here it just turns gray, and not a nice gray like your brothers, but this dirty color. No fear, we'll get you cleaned up at the Stallburg.* Ah, here we come up to the Belvedere Palace and gardens—not looking their best this time of year, but still . . ."

I was too amazed by the people and cars to take much note of the particular sights he mentioned, but his steady patter was soothing. The wide roads, the strange statuary, the sweep and breadth of this man-made landscape were marvelous and slightly terrifying. The mingling of trees and orderly plants—not, as the groom noted, looking their best in very early spring—with the enormous white buildings fronted by gravel drives and fountains was such a combination of nature and craft to make a horse quite confused. Did we really belong here? In a place where, it seemed, we were the lone animals, except for small barking dogs straining at their leads to get a better look at us?

"The Schwarzenberggarten starts here . . . we'll pass the palace soon . . . here's the trolley ringing its bell for you—easy there, old boy. Nothing to worry about. Just another sort of train, on wires. We'll cross over to a quieter street now. Ah, smell that? Coffee. I have a passion for it. Strudel, too. I have as big of a sweet tooth as you

---

* The stable

horses. I'll bring you a bit of apple strudel and you can try it. We won't tell the others."

And so our procession continued, past palaces and royal gardens, museums and libraries, cafés and apartment buildings, all cheerfully described by the slim, long-legged boy beside me. He smelled of sugar and damp wool and horses, and his voice, though pitched higher than Jan's, was pleasant. In front of me, Ned and Pluto Adrina seemed to be enjoying themselves, though Ned was impatient with our pace, kept necessarily slow by the uncertain footing of the wet streets and the uneven cobblestones we occasionally hazarded.

As I became calmer and more in control of all the strange sensations of the city, I started to notice more. The smell of coffee—I recognized it by the third café we passed—bracing, earthy, and comfortable. The size and shape of people and the number of ladies . . . far more than I had ever seen before. The ladies often went with the small dogs. The smell of damp fur from the ladies' coats, the smell of smoke from the chimneys. The queer smell of the trolley—like lightning. And then I couldn't help but notice the effect we seemed to have on the people we passed. At first, their sheer number had made them incomprehensible—they were no more than a noisy crowd. But twenty minutes into our procession, I could tell how much attention we attracted. Men and women peered at us from windows, waved to us from the trolleys, honked the horns of their cars (which made the grooms cross). Pedestrians made way for us, smiling broadly and sounding soft *oohs* and *ahhs*. Behind me was a herd of children keeping as close to us as they dared, and frequently being hushed and shooed by our grooms. After about the fourth scolding, the children in front quieted down and marched solemnly along, taking it upon themselves to hush and scold all of the new children who came skipping up to join the parade.

All this, apparently, was for us. Had they never seen a horse before?

"See, Schnecki?" said my groom. "You're famous already. Everyone loves the horses of *Die Spanische*. You'll have an audience every time you train and little faces waiting to get a peep at you when you go back to the Stallburg. You'll have to get used to living in the limelight."

Just then the sun came out from behind the clouds and lit the scene before me with a cheerful glow. It was impossible to resist: the brightening day, the happy faces

around me, the excited whispers of the children, the respect and awe that we obviously excited. I picked up
my feet and arched my neck, feeling strength and health
flow through me from my head to my quarters. It didn't
matter that I was splashed up to my hocks with slush or
that my tail was quite bedraggled. My groom's hand was
steady on my lead and we walked well together. I felt–
proud. I found the city beautiful and its inhabitants friends
already. I suddenly knew that I was, indeed, home.

And what a home it was. If there hadn't been a distinct horsey smell coming from the graceful white walls
of the lofty buildings on either side of me, I would have
assumed they were just two more palaces like the others
my groom had pointed out. But this, apparently, was our
actual residence. The neighing beyond the walls con-
firmed it. I stared up at the swooping archways, felt all
the strange man-made-ness of it all. Had they built a
palace just for horses? Would the wonders of this day
never cease?

We stopped for a moment, then turned into a kind
of paddock, though like none I had ever seen before. It
was lined with stone, and our hooves rang out as we
stepped through the tall wooden doorway of the en-
trance into the courtyard. Creamy white walls arose on

all four sides of this central expanse of stone, but they were less walls than another series of arches, as graceful and regular as the trees of Piber, and stamped out like horseshoes all in a row. The sky above this enclosure was a dome of soft blue. The noise and bustle of the city receded as the doors shut behind us; indeed, it was remarkably peaceful here, at least in contrast to the trolleys and small dogs.

It was far from still—there was plenty of activity to be seen and heard, but it was all horse-related activity, familiar and understandable. I caught a glimpse of a groom mucking out a stall, heard the rumble of a wheelbarrow, smelled oats and hay and other horses. I saw Dr. Besel, the stud's manager, shaking hands with a man I recognized as Director Graf, and heard the clicking of cameras, which reminded me of the people who visited Piber and the fuss they made over us. *Really, we've always been fussed over,* I thought to myself, trying to observe the Director more closely. *Perhaps here I'll find out why.*

Ned, of course, required no explanation. He looked absolutely delighted with our reception and was busy pawing the stones (to no effect), announcing his presence with authority. Pluto Adrina looked around for fillies and, finding none, hunted in his groom's pocket for more sugar. I tried to sidle over to Ned, but my groom prevented the movement, kindly but firmly. The men talked for a little longer, we were patted in both welcome and good-bye, and then we were led through one of the innumerable archways to discover where in a palace a horse might sleep.

CHAPTER 4

"**I HOPE YOU'RE NOT NOISY. MY LAST NEIGHBOR** slobbered his oats so dreadfully it quite put me off my feed. Try to practice a modicum of restraint during meals, young stallion. There is nothing worse than attempting to enjoy a quiet meal while being assaulted by the sounds of a horse doing his best imitation of a pig."

My neighbor stared balefully at me for a moment. I stared back, unsure what, if anything, I should say. Perhaps I could simply refrain from slobbering and that would give him confidence. He was an absolutely noble old stallion, nearly a full hand shorter than I, but with an air and authority that made him seem much taller. His snowy neck was as finely curved as any of my new home's characteristic arches, and his thick white mane hung in soft waves down his neck. His eyes were a glistening, intelligent black, his ears tiny and pointed, and even his large pink nostrils seemed dainty. He was also the cleanest horse I had ever seen in my life. He was, in short, the kind of horse who should be eating his oats from a red marble basin, with which all of our stalls were equipped.

The marble basin was only one of the wonders of the Stallburg. All of the fittings of my roomy box stall were different from the ones in the barns at Piber—more worn, perhaps, but comfortable, with the straw fetlock-deep, a salt lick nestled in the corner, the bars on two sides nicely spaced for a muzzle touch. The front of the stall, above the dark wood paneling, opened onto a narrow, crooked corridor that wove between the rows of white and dappled gray (and occasionally brown) horse heads. More astonishing was the fact that I had a window carved into the wall above me, and by the window a sort of frozen, white horse head grew out of the wall, which curved, of course, into the arch that formed the ceiling of this horse palace. The whole building was snug on a horsey scale and yet grand in a human way, and that seemed appropriate from what I had seen so far of how life in Vienna was styled for a Lipizzaner.

Hearing no response, my neighbor turned his hindquarters to me in a pointed fashion. Through the opposite bars I could hear Ned, thankfully my other neighbor, making a loud acquaintance with the horse on his other side:

"Great hall, this one! We call it the Royal Wee, 'cause, y'know, they pick up our straw as soon as we have a pee. The stallions in the other two halls say they get the same treatment, but I've seen some dirty coronets, swear on my dam's forelock. Anyway, what's your name?"

"Ned, what's yours?"

"Heck, you're not Ned anymore. That's a farm nickname. What's your full name? Mine's Conversano Bonadea, and my rider calls me 'Bonadea,' and my groom calls me 'Bonny.' That's how nicknames go around here—by your mother's name. I mean, back at Piber they called me *Witzbold*,* but obviously I've outgrown that."

"Oh, well, I'm Neapolitano Galanta. . . ."

"So you'll be 'Galanta' or maybe just 'Galant.' See?"

Ned apparently did see, and saw no reason to further question his abrupt change of name, for the conversation moved to the topic of our hay and its superior quality to the hay served in other halls. But I was flummoxed. Ned was no longer Ned? And was I no longer Schnecki? Was I also Galanta, or Galant? I wouldn't mind sharing a name with Ned, though I imagined it might lead to some confusion. But then—no. Galanta might for all intents and purposes be my dam, but I did not share

---

* Joker

her name with her natural son. Of course, I bore my birth mother's name. I was Favory Mercurio. They would be calling me *Mercurio*.

I was horrified. To lose my nickname—familiar and dear as it was—was bad enough. But I could bear trading it for something else—perhaps simply *Ned's brother.* Instead I would be shackled with the constant reminder of the shame of my past, of my dam's rejection. It was a mockery to be called by the very name of the horse that despised me, that would probably be outraged if she knew. How could I make a new beginning under this cloud, this humiliation? And once the other horses found out I had been spurned at birth and discovered the irony of my nickname, they would torment me, I was sure. There was a cocky air to Ned's neighbor, Bonny, and a sense of competition in the air. We were, after all, thirty-five or so stallions all lodged one on top of the other in three lengths of corridor crooked as a rabbit's warren. Life would be miserable if they ganged up on me. For where would I go? There were no hills . . . no mountains . . . no escape.

"You look unhappy."

I jumped. My other neighbor had swung his hind-quarters back around and was now sniffing at me through the bars. His expression was stern, as if he were personally offended by my lack of spirits.

"It's just a bit crowded," I muttered.

The old stallion snorted dismissively. "Oh yes, that's what all the first years say. I want to *run*, I want to *play*. It is time to put childish things away, young stallion. You are here to learn. To work. To become great."

I let the obvious question–become great at *what*?–lie for the moment. I wondered if the old stallion, who had years of experience under the arches of *Die Spanische*, could shed any light on my dreaded new name.

"I was just overhearing that our riders call us . . . some sort of nickname?" I snuffed around in my hay, keeping my face averted.

"I wouldn't call it a 'nickname' per se." He snorted again. He had a most emphatic snort, and I was soon to discover that it was the backbone on which most of his conversation hung. "A 'convenient abridgement' would be more appropriate. There are only six classical stallion lines and, of course, quite a number more mare lines and mare names available, so for the sake of contraction the stallion's second name is preferred, otherwise we'd have seven Plutos trotting about and ten Maestosos, etc. It's only a matter of common sense."

"And it's not strange that suddenly we are called ... mares' names? Our mothers'?" My nervousness must have been apparent, for the old stallion replied most pointedly.

"Not if you're quite secure with your masculinity."

I don't know what's worse—being called "Mercurio" or having my stallionhood challenged by a short old bully in the next stall, I thought.

I lifted my head high at his challenge and looked down at him with what I hoped was an expression of supreme unconcern. I arched my tail a bit and settled my hindquarters squarely. Schnecki I might be, but I had my pride.

"My name is Favory Mercurio," I said.

"And I am Siglavy Strana. Pleased to make your acquaintance, young stallion." The old horse's eyes twinkled up at me, obviously delighted that he had provoked me so successfully.

"So you are called 'Strana'?" I asked.

The blast of a snort I received told me I'd stepped in it again.

"They call me *Maestro.* You're quite welcome for cheering you up." With that, Siglavy Strana—the Maestro—turned his hindquarters back in my face and fell asleep.

. . .

THERE WAS LITTLE SLEEP FOR ME THAT NIGHT.
The chattering neighs and whistles of a dozen stallions
rang up and down the corridors intermittently—everyone
seemed excited by our arrival and most felt the need to
announce their own position in the school, which was
truly one large herd. Our hall—the Royal Wee—was a
mixture of mature school stallions (who were uniformly
quiet and slept soundly) and younger stallions in either
their first or second stages of training (they were the
noisy, self-announcing group). And there was something
different about sleeping in a city, without the usual
nighttime chorus of crickets and wind in the trees. The
city sounds were not obtrusive, but still there was a distinct feeling that outside these walls was not Nature but
Man. So despite the comfort of my stall and the excel-
lence of my supper, I was restless, nervous, and more
than a little claustrophobic. Even when the last snorts
and grumbles and jeers died down and a heavy quiet
settled over the Stallburg, I stood alert, eyes wide to the
half-dimness around me. That was another difference:
The barn was never fully dark, not the deep dark of winter nights in the mountains.

By morning I was tired, stiff from standing in one

position for so long, and feeling very homesick. I greeted Ned through the bars of our adjoining stalls and could smell the excitement coursing through him.

"Some place!" He pawed his straw enthusiastically. "Wonder when we get breakfast? Wonder what we do today? Wonder who our groom will be?"

"Not groom—*élève*,"* Bonny interrupted. "You'll get assigned an élève. All the first years do. I'm a third year—just got advanced to the *campagne*, or lower school, and my élève got promoted to assistant rider already. Couple more years in the campagne and then High School. Can't wait for High School. My sire was a champion capriole performer and everyone expects big things from me, I can tell you." Bonny broke off to chug some water from his basin, giving Ned the opportunity to say what I was wholeheartedly thinking:

"*What* in the name of Pegasus are you talking about?"

Bonny chuckled into his basin, bubbling water over the sides. "No worries," he said with a snort (not as elegantly as the Maestro). "You'll pick up the lingo soon enough. Besides, all you have to do for the next week is run around and sleep and eat. Hey, here they come!"

---

* Trainee

I pricked my ears at the sound of men's voices approaching. I was pleased to see my guide of yesterday, and very glad that it was his hand at the door of my stall, rumpling my forelock and saying in a kind voice, "Good morning, old fellow. I bet you'd like to move around a bit, wouldn't you?" I very much did, and I snuffled his sleeve and fingers with as much enthusiasm as I could muster, given the state of my taut nerves.

"You are fortunate," Maestro commented through the bars. "Young Max is a fine boy. Take in his scent and tell me what you find."

I took a few deep breaths, tasting the air, Young Max's hands, and then rubbed my muzzle on his chest. I didn't know what Maestro expected me to discover; all I could smell was the boy's flavor of wool and sugar, snow and apples, and a kind of warm, woodsy scent that reminded me of home, though I couldn't quite place it with anything from Piber. Then Max dug into his pocket and pulled out a small, indeterminate lump, which he offered to me. It smelled like the cafés we had passed the day before—sweet and spicy. It melted on my tongue almost the instant it was in my mouth, leaving behind an exquisite taste of apples and autumn.

"Strudel." Max winked at me. "I told you you'd like it!"

"Max, if you are giving that baby strudel already, you'll spoil him before his first week is up," came a teasing voice from down the hall.

"And how is it different from all the sugar, eh?"

"Because next he'll want a cup of coffee and a newspaper," the unseen élève retorted, and the sound of quiet laughter skipped up and down the corridor. It was a pleasant sound. Between the lingering bits of cinnamon and apple on my tongue, the cheerful voices of the young men, and Max's homey smell, I was feeling considerably better.

"I don't know what he's supposed to smell like," I remarked to Maestro, "but I like the strudel very much."

"Oh, well." The old horse sighed. "I thought you might find him familiar. We are all linked by the blood of empire, in various ways. Your founding sire, Favory, was born in the Imperial Stud of Kladruby, in Bohemia.* Hundreds of years ago of course. But Young Max is from the same part of the world, on his dam's side. By the

---

* Part of the present-day Czech Republic, in Central Europe

great river Elbe. As is *Oberbereiter* Polak, the greatest man here."

There was no time to make further inquiries into the odd notion that my élève, the greatest man at *Die Spanische*, and I all somehow came from one stud farm in a place I'd never heard of, for Max was leading me out of my stall, in the wake of Ned and a handful of other horses.

"Have fun!" Bonny called. "If you see Slava, give him a kick in the hindquarters for me. I hate that guy."

"Sure!" Ned trumpeted back, ready, as always, for anything, even if it involved picking a fight with a total stranger. "But where are we going?"

"To the *Winterreitschule*, freshie! Fanciest paddock you'll ever see! Just don't poop where the emperor can see you!"

The last thing I heard as we made our way toward the door was the distinct snort of Maestro telling Bonny to shut his muzzle.

CHAPTER 5

I**F BONNY HADN'T CHARACTERIZED THE** *Winterreitschule* as a paddock, I would never in a thousand years have thought it was a place built for horses. But it was no more a "paddock" than one of the wild mountainsides of Western Styria was a "pasture."

In fact, I thought, this could be a kind of human version of the grandeur of the snowy peaks of home. I blinked up at the flood of daylight that poured into the fantastical white hall, illuminating the elaborate frozen shapes that seemed to me like so many delicate drifts of ice and snow, suspended in time like the white horse head above my stall. The very sky was white and carved in floes and veins like a snow-covered waterfall, and a silence and peace reigned here, as they reigned in the wintery, snowbound hollows between the hills of Piber. It was a sunny dome, a cave of ice, with a slash of red in the very center of the far wall, like a cardinal on a winter tree.

And suddenly this silent winter palace was filled with horses, none of whom seemed overawed by the grandeur of the place. Snorting, pawing, and taking great, energetic strides into the center of the arena, five stallions rushed by me as I stood, dazzled, by the door. They broke the spell, and I bounded forward to join them, eager, for once, to simply run around with a bunch of horses. It felt so good to loosen and stretch my tense muscles that I lost my head and bucked down the entire long side of the arena, then took a few bouncing leaps as if I were jumping over the mountain streams of home. I shook my head and tossed my forelock and pranced happily around the corners—until I felt an unceremonious kick on my flank. It was hard, and it hurt.

"Out of my way, first year," snorted a well-muscled, dapple gray stallion, apparently the giver of the kick. His neck snaked viciously forward, and he got right up in my muzzle. "We're running *this* way. Stay with the herd." His ears were pinned so tightly back to his skull that they appeared to be missing altogether. He had a very long, narrow face, and his stone gray forelock parted in a dark curtain over his eyes. I glanced behind him. The herd didn't seem to be going in any particular direction. Everywhere I looked, I saw frolicking, bantering stallions, play fighting, smelling one another, getting annoyed and lashing out, jostling for position in front of the group. Nothing I hadn't seen at Piber, after all.

"The herd seems fine without me," I ventured, and eased away from the threatening face now pressing even closer to my own. The stranger seemed to want to shove me backward into the corner, trapping me, and after allowing myself to be forced back a few steps, I decided this was not the best idea. I sidestepped, swinging my hindquarters away from the wall, and tried to get my head over the gray's. I failed spectacularly: The stallion reared, batting at my neck with his forelegs, and I squealed in protest. At the sound, a groom materialized just ahead of us, waving my attacker off with a sharp word and emphatic gestures.

"Tattletale," the stallion snorted at me with an evil look as he turned, reluctantly, away. "Mama's boy." That cheered me up. He might have rattled me a little, but I knew for a fact that I was no mama's boy.

The rest of our frolic in the *Winterreitschule* passed in relative peace, though it passed too quickly. I felt I could have wandered around the long oval, studying the light, the people watching us from the balconies, the elaborate snowy world within its walls, for quite a bit longer. I also wanted more freedom. I wanted to walk through the streets of Vienna with Max, have more strudel, find some grass perhaps just now peeking through melted snow. I was restless, filled with a yearning for more . . . more of everything, I suppose. More room, more time, and more answers as to what I was supposed to be, and how I would become it. I was reluctant to leave the arena, but Max did not force me. He waited until I was ready, until I knew that no matter how much I'd rather stay, I'd still have to go, and it wasn't worth fighting about. Then, as I finally stepped forward, toward him, he gave me his last bit of strudel, as if in consolation.

. . .

"SO THAT WAS SLAVA?" I CALLED OVER TO Bonny as we ate our hay back in the Stallburg. "The one with the skinny face and negative attitude?"

"That's the one," Bonny said, putting his ears back. "Did you kick him for me?"

"No—he kicked me, though. I think I hate that guy."

"We all do, Mercury. We all hate that guy." Bonny sighed heavily.

"Hey!" Ned broke in. "Is that your new name? Is that what they're calling you now?"

"Um, I don't know. Is it, Bonny?" *Mercury*. It wasn't quite as bad as Mercurio, somehow. It sounded almost the same of course, but there was perhaps enough of a difference ... *Mercury*. I tried it out in my head. It wasn't ... awful.

"That's what I heard Max the Gypsy call you, when you all were in the *Winterreitschule*. He said he wanted to give the little snail wings, whatever that means."

"Young Max was referring to *Merkur*, or Mercury—or Hermes, for that matter—god of the ancients, in an empire even before the Hapsburgs." I had assumed Maestro was asleep, but I was soon to learn that one of his many skills was feigning unconsciousness. Perhaps it wasn't entirely deliberate; he seemed to exist very comfortably in a twilight state, musing his own inscrutable thoughts, not bothering with the rest of us unless something piqued his attention, as it had now.

"Mind explaining that, sir?" Bonny said in the habitually respectful and affectionate manner with which all the stallions treated my neighbor.

"A god. A human god. Not the creator of horses—no, that was Poseidon for the Greeks, Neptune after the Romans got hold of him. Always seemed strange to have horses born from water, especially the ocean. It's not our best medium. But, ah, Mercury has a hat with wings. God of messengers, dreams, thieves, and, well, a few more things I'm sure. You'll see Greeks and Romans scattered throughout the city . . . Theseus in the Volksgarten, Athena outside the Parliament building. They, too, are part of our history. All of Europe is. We are citizens of the world."

And with that, Maestro really fell asleep.

. . .

IF THE FOLLOWING WEEKS DID NOT BRING enlightenment as to our purpose in Vienna, they did at least bring a measure of resignation to our new lifestyle. Gradually I got used to the schedule of meals, meticulous grooming, and daily frolics in the *Winterreitschule*, became acquainted with the stallions of our hall and the second years who ran with us under the white dome of the snowy palace. I had several more run-ins with Slava–his kind of bullying was impossible to avoid altogether–but as I merely resisted him, instead of challenging him, he eventually lost interest in me.

"See?" Ned told me one morning, "You're already Uncle Mercury here, like you were Uncle Schnecki at Piber. Everyone trusts you and knows to leave you alone when you want it."

I had to admit he had a point. I had always thought of myself as a loner, bound only to Ned and to Jan, aloof from the herd. But there was no luxury of escape here, except mental. I was forced to live cheek by jowl with a slew of strangers, and to my surprise, they both accepted me and let me be, allowing me to carve out a space of liberty, at least in my own head. And, so far, no one had remarked on either my looks or my mother.

"Who would want to mess with Mercury?" Bonny asked incredulously. "I mean, he'll never be perfect, like me, or boss of the first years, but he's, well, *smart*. Total brain."

"Thanks, Bonny," I said modestly, licking my block of salt. Yes, it took the sting out of our confinement, being respected by the others. Pluto Adrina had not had such luck—he and Slava seemed enmeshed in daily guerrilla warfare in the *Winterreitschule*, and he did not get along well with his neighbors down the corridor. I had always thought he was a bold horse, though filly-obsessed. The others apparently thought he was a bit of a blowhard. Ned—Ned was Ned, though now Galant. Brave, spirited, cheerful, and a great social creature. I suspected I owed half of my unexpected cachet to his good offices, though of course he denied it.

My élève, Max, was a regular presence, and soon an eagerly expected one. He couldn't have been more different from Jan—dark where Jan was fair, long-legged and thin where Jan was stocky, and sober where Jan was smiling. But I liked people, and Max was my person. More—he suited me. He had great dark eyes set in a melancholy face, and his movements and voice were always quiet and calm. He appeared to have taken Jan's parting words quite to heart and was never impatient or rude to me. He gave simple instructions over and over again, waiting patiently until I understood. And he seemed to like me. I've always responded well to people who like me.

By my third week at *Die Spanische*, I felt I understood what, so far, was expected of me. And so then, of course it all changed.

I remembered saddles and bridles from Piber, though it had been a while since I'd worn them, so I didn't object when Max suited me up one morning, especially when I saw Ned's élève, Georg, doing the same. The bit was a light snaffle, and Max didn't cinch the girth too tight, so I felt comfortable and interested in the change of routine.

"And so it begins," Maestro commented, eyes half closed. "You have wondered what your purpose is, young stallion, and today is the first step on the road to discovery and understanding."

It was thrilling. I could hardly stand still as Max finished his adjustments and plucked a stray piece of straw from my tail. I caught Ned's eye and we exchanged excited glances. *And so it begins!*

And twenty-five minutes later, it ended.

Ned was frankly disgusted. "All we got to do was walk around in a circle for twenty minutes? Seriously? I got a good canter up and Georg just stared at me with this sort of sad look on his face until I walked again, and then he gave me a ridiculous amount of sugar. OK, I get it. Walk in a circle. Get sugar. But what's the *point*?"

I was wondering the same thing. It had taken me longer to figure out what Max wanted than it had taken Ned, of course, but it seemed as though a minute after I stopped walking back over to Max and had gone around in a few circles like he wanted, he put a halt to the proceedings, showered me with praise, and called it a day. It was, truly, a little embarrassing.

"Every great artistic endeavor has a beginning, and this is ours." I had had a feeling we were coming home to a lecture from Maestro, and I was right. "You must learn to walk. To trot, especially. You must learn to understand the riders."

"I know how to walk," Ned grumbled.

"Do you, Neapolitano Galanta? Do you know how to correctly place your hoofs, to bend the body, to align your hindquarters with your shoulders, and to free your back?"

"Erm–"

"Did you buck?"

"Once or twice, maybe."

"Did you gallop?"

"Well . . . only a little."

"Did you wander aimlessly toward your élève, or the other horses?"

"That was Mercury, not me."

"The beginning of wisdom is to first accept how little you know. And you two, I'm afraid, know nothing. Do not feel ashamed. It is how we all begin."

Fine, I thought. *But if this was the beginning, what would be our end?* First I must walk in a circle. Or should I say, learn a new way of walking in a circle. No, that wasn't right either. Learn a new way of *thinking* about walking in a circle?

"My brain hurts," I commented aloud. I directed the complaint toward Ned, but it was Maestro who answered.

"And that is *exactly* the muscle you should be exercising, young stallion," he said in a satisfied tone.

CHAPTER 6

APPARENTLY NED AND I DID KNOW HOW TO walk, and yet we needed to learn how to walk under a new set of circumstances.

It's easy, with the benefit of hindsight, to follow the stages of our training and see how one accomplishment—athletic or intellectual—led to another challenge, never too little to bore us or too big to defeat us. But I am talking in riddles. Let me see if I can explain better than Maestro—the master of mysterious pronouncement—ever did.

I am a horse, a Lipizzaner, a stallion. I have gaits (very nice ones): walk, trot, canter, gallop. I naturally made use of these gaits in the early part of my life, those halcyon days in the fields and mountains and paddocks of Piber. What I was to learn in my first year at *Die Spanische* was to walk, trot, and canter naturally—but with a rider, under longe lines, or in hand, and with all the equipment that entails. At first, you can't help changing: a bridle and bit exert pressure, a saddle with a man in it is quite heavy, longe lines create tension, however light-handed. Your body adjusts to all these things, and so do your gaits and movements. The trick is to adjust in a way that is most like what your gaits and movements would be if you had no rider, no equipment, no burdens at all!

It took me some time to learn this. There are all sorts of reactions you can have to the feelings of being ridden, from hunching your back to dragging your feet to getting under the bit (a particular problem of mine) to developing stiffness on one side of your body (in my case, the right). But you do not compensate for these issues by learning something new, some trick or strategy . . . you must address them by becoming, if anything, more natural, more horselike. It takes grace to accept this much interference and to act as if you weren't being interfered with at all. But luckily you have a rider who is mostly helping you, though at first it's hard to tell because you're getting used to so many new sensations. Then after a while you do get the feeling that the person in the saddle or holding the lines is there to support you, not to confuse you, and once that happens the mental magic—so key to our training—has been performed: You've made common cause with this human, and suddenly his project is your project, and the project is *you.*

I doubt I've explained that any better than Maestro. There is something about life and training at *Die Spanische* that lends itself to enigmatic speeches, no matter how straightforward the actual exercises are. *Oberbereiter* Polak used to refer to the alchemical process of riding, saying that horse and rider combined together to make a new creature, a new substance. The Colonel, when he came, called it the "secret speech" shared between man and horse. Whatever poetry you want to make of it (and the entire place lends itself to poetry), here are some scenes from our first years, which should serve better than words to describe what it was all about.

· · ·

WHEN I FIRST MET *OBERBEREITER* POLAK AGAIN, I thought he was the god referred to in my new nickname, the one with wings on his hat. But once I looked past his impressive headgear, I saw the face that had seemed so familiar during the final *Musterung** at Piber, when it was decided that I was fit for training at the school.

---

* Inspection

"Well now," he murmured as he petted my che and looked me calmly in the eye, "here is a horse wh knows who he is."

It was a strange time to make this remark, as I was just learning to ride under the saddle with Max, and while I'd gained a certain amount of confidence in following my élève's aides, I was still teased (gently) with being a slowpoke. The general consensus was that Ned and even Pluto Adrina were much farther along than I was. I was surprised now when Max agreed with the Chief Rider.

"Yes, we may call him 'Mercury,' but he is still Schnecki," he said. "He has not advanced as far as the others, it's true, but it is remarkable how little he forgets. His faults are never disobedience—they are in trying to understand correctly."

"I cannot think of a higher compliment," Polak replied, giving me a final pat. "And as I was the one to give him the nickname Schnecki during one of my visits to the stud, I'm not displeased that it still suits him. Come. Show me what you both have learned."

This conversation took place in the Stallburg, as there was very little talking in the *Winterreitschule*, and all of that done by the instructors, none by the élèves.

Well, Max talked (quietly) to me, but never to Polak or to the other senior riders who formed our community of trainers.

Today we were continuing our work on my stiff right side. Max often squeezed the reins while still asking, through his legs and seat, for me to move forward, and this made me adjust my contact on the bit until he seemed satisfied. Apparently, though I'd never realized it, I was a little crooked in my movements, and this needed to be adjusted every day.

"You are overdoing it, Max," Polak admonished in a just-audible murmur from the center of the ring. Immediately, the squeezing lessened, and I readjusted my head.

"Ahem. Underdoing it, I'm afraid. Go large* and try again."

Max guided me back to the long wall of the school and this time we went around the entire outside track, meeting and passing Bonny, who was doing voltes† in the corner.

"Good to see the Maestro hasn't forgotten his tricks." Bonny winked at me as I trotted by. Startled, I turned

---

* Around the full arena
† Small circles

my head to the center of the ring, searching out my neighbor among the white bodies moving more or less harmoniously in various formations around the school. I could tell Max was chagrined by my sudden distraction—my nose had swung up and I was trotting quicker than he liked—but I had literally never seen Maestro out of his stall, except occasionally in fine weather, when we were walked together in the courtyard, or *Sommerreitschule.* I knew he still trained (or rather, trained young riders himself) and still performed the quadrille, but I'd never seen it, nor seen him do anything other than walk (which he did beautifully) or lecture (which he did at length) or sleep (which he did almost as well as he walked). I felt aflame with curiosity.

And then I spotted him. He was tied between the twin white pillars where a form of advanced training was conducted that I did not fully understand. But then, my ideas about the pillars had mostly been formed by a dramatic and upsetting incident in which a stallion, apparently not ready to be initiated to these mysteries, tried to pull himself out from the ties and to take his three trainers down with him. I had avoided thinking about them ever since. But now, as I slowed my trot to take a good look at my elderly neighbor, I saw the pillars in an entirely new light. I saw them as the frames for something so beautiful that I stopped in my tracks, nearly unsettling Max. But I had to stop: The Maestro was dancing!

He was trotting, if this springy, floating, dancing rhythm could be called a trot, but he wasn't moving forward, and not because the pillars' ties were holding him back. No, he was holding himself back, creating a kind of loop of action: motion that flowed forward, only to be arrested, like a frozen waterfall. This gait, or dance movement, was familiar, too: It was the illustration of excitement, pride, longing. As a yearling, you would call it prancing in place. As a senior stallion, Maestro was executing the piaffe. His eyes shone with delight as he swayed rhythmically from legs to legs—his very forelock bristled with pride. I was amazed by the power of his hindquarters, how far they reached under his belly, and how much weight they bore to free his forelegs. This was not merely lovely—this required strength, stamina, and focus. The more I watched, the more impressed I was.

And then, at an invisible signal from the man standing beside him, and as if it were the most natural thing in the world, Maestro stopped, waited a few beats, then rose up on those magnificent hind legs and became as much of a statue as any of the snow sculptures above our heads. In fact, it was at that moment, when the fine old stallion executed his renowned levade, holding perfectly still with his elegant forelegs tucked neatly before him, that something of the connection between this place, the *Winterreitschule*, and our work as horses and with men came together for me. My feelings were jumbled, but I could sense the relationship between Maestro's pose and the ageless school, with its elaborate sky and hushed atmosphere, the endless patience of the men and the slow, measured pace of our days. Suddenly I knew that I was part of something greater than myself. And if this place, this palace of horses, was housed in the cosmopolitan heart of Europe, then what we did must matter even to the people beyond our walls. After all, they came to see us every day, lining the balcony and peering down at us. I had often wondered what they were looking for, or what exactly they saw when they stared at us. Now, staring myself at Maestro, I thought I understood.

"Let him look," came a quiet voice by my shoulder. I was surprised to see Polak there; I hadn't even noticed his approach. Poor Max, I could feel his anxiety that I was being so disobedient during our first ride before the

Oberbereiter. But he could not defend or explain from the saddle—he had been reprimanded for this before. He sat, stiff with embarrassment, radiating annoyance through the reins.

"It is absolutely right that he should be interested in his neighbor's actions. Of course, we cannot allow him to be so distracted by other horses in general, but if he wants to watch Maestro perform, he could not have a better example to follow." Max relaxed, and I continued to study the movements of the grand stallion between the pillars.

Later, back in the Stallburg, he asked me, "Mercury, were you actually learning something from Maestro, or were you just messing about?" He laughed. "Myself, I think you were messing about. Glad Polak had another explanation, though!"

"That might be the least intelligent thing I've heard Young Max say," Maestro remarked in a sour tone.

· · ·

LOOKING BACK, THAT AFTERNOON WAS A TURN-ing point in my training. Between the example of Maestro and the introduction of *Oberbereiter* Polak as our primary instructor, a threshold had been crossed for both Max and me. By the end of my second year at *Die*

Spanische, we were making steady progress—progress I could feel in the strengthening of my body, in the increasing suppleness of my joints, and in the way I thought about our exercises and how best to perform them. I was no longer an ignorant first year; now I did my best to provide a buffer for the new horses sent up from Piber against the new generation of bullies (Pluto Adrina, among them, I'm afraid). Slava and Bonny still butted heads, but Bonny had bigger things on his mind than fighting with another stallion, however provoking. As he had long hoped for and predicted, Bonny was following in his father's hoofprints and was being trained as a capriole artist.

Ned was quite desperate to master the capriole, too. We had watched Bonny launching through the air (some attempts more successful than others) in this most beautiful and dramatic of the Airs Above the Ground, as the advanced movements were called. Ned wanted to fly—and if any horse could fly, I was sure it would be Ned. I had no particular ambition, except to please Max and *Oberbereiter* Polak. These two, plus Ned and to some extent Maestro and Bonny, had my heart.

They worked in concert, and their different energies were quite engrossing. Max, like me, was young, eager, and intense. Polak, who started riding me occasionally at the end of my second year, was unflappable. I felt excited trying new things with Max, and I felt like a genius when Polak was in the saddle. His aids were so clear, his seat so calm, his spirit so encouraging—well, I'm raving. But he was a rider, and a dear man, worth raving about.

By the end of my second year, I was ready to graduate to the campagne for my third year of training. Ned graduated with me, and so did Pluto Adrina. It's true that they always outpaced me in learning new movements and exercises, but somehow, perhaps through my sheer persistence, or perhaps because the other two had a tendency to backslide, we usually ended up at about the same level. Which meant, at this point, that we could walk, trot, and canter in a straight and forward fashion, under a rider. More, we could perform all these gaits with a degree of collection as well. My collection, if I do say so myself, was good. Pluto Adrina's was not—he had weak hindquarters—but he was such a nice mover overall that his élève, Stefan, had high (and boastful, to my ears) hopes for him. Ned had flashes of brilliance, but he was erratic, and he and his élève, Georg—high-spirited, forever whistling—were a volatile combination. In comparison with these four bouncing, proud boys, Max and I were a sober pair indeed: dark where they were fair, quiet where they were rowdy, and deliberate where they were charging full steam ahead. It didn't matter. They seemed rather to love us, just as we were.

I had started to learn the piaffe, and was working on my passage. I had learned to bend my body in a number of ways, and to place my feet with deliberate care. I had watched the few stallions who could perform the Airs Above the Ground . . . the flying capriole, the gravity-defying courbette, the Maestro's levade. According to Maestro, these movements, besides being formalized versions of what stallions did naturally, had their roots in warfare, both horse and human.

"Never forget that our exercises—no matter how elegant, how artistic—have been formed by the partnership of horses and humans in battle," he told me seriously. "What is the capriole but a form of evasion? What is my levade but a posture to strike down one's enemies from above? Or, in our terms, what is a courbette but an aggressive challenge to a stallion making an incursion on one's territory?"

War. A stallion understood it instinctively, of course—

even me. I was no Slava, no Pluto Adrina, but we are born with a need for rank, for mares, and for ownership of a place. In the world that humans have made for us, these needs—molded, necessarily, by our circumstances— are expressed differently, but they still exist. Some stallions boss other stallions. Some stallions boss the humans that take care of them. Some become followers. Some become possessive of the space around them, creating a territory wherever they trot. Some, like me, put a human at the head of their ranking system. Max was my general, my alpha, and I had a feeling that if ever called upon, I would carry him into battle without blinking an eye. I wish, in many ways, that I could have.

CHAPTER 7

THE SPRING OF 1939 WAS REMARKABLY BEAU-
tiful. The heavy, sweet smell of the chestnut trees
perfumed the *Sommerreitschule* during our evening strolls,
and the doves and blackbirds whirled in the fragile
gray-blue of the evening sky. I loved when it was our
turn in the courtyard—we trained there, too, of course,
but I especially prized my hours of liberty, surrounded
by the timeless arches. I had my own fancies, my own
memories, though their clarity faded with each passing
year at *Die Spanische*. I liked to conjure up the feeling of
solitude I had relished on my mountainside. I had little
chance, in my new life, to maintain the position I most
preferred: that of belonging to a herd, and to people,
but having the luxury to observe them from some dis-
tance. To not *mix* so much, to put it bluntly. Here I was
forced into community—a community I mostly loved, to
be sure, but still . . . there were moments when I very
much wished to be by myself.

71

Horses do not like change. We are sentimental and steadfast, stubborn and of limited imagination. We prefer safety, routine, and a comfortable amount of freedom. To a certain degree, we can be made to fight cavalry charges as long as we have our familiar brush and a bucket of oats—on the other hand, we can become neurotics. It comes down to trust. I trusted Max and *Oberbereiter* Polak, and I loved a handful of the horses in my stable, so there was little chance I would turn sour. More, I usually found our near-daily forty-five-minute training sessions invigorating. I had bad days, to be sure, but Max was so scrupulously careful to end our sessions on a good note—in essence, to restore my pride even when I had bungled badly—that my low moods never lasted long.

Other horses did not fare as well. I've spoken of the psychological transformations that were such necessary ingredients to our training: making common cause with our riders, making peace with our elegant confinement. Over the course of my early years at *Die Spanische*, I witnessed a handful of transformations gone awry, or made incompletely . . . or not at all. Some stallions simply couldn't be brought on board, so to speak, and they expressed their unsuitableness for life at the school in ways ranging from the emphatic (throwing riders, fighting with other horses) to the quiet (going off their feed, becoming dull and listless). These horses were not allowed to remain miserable—they were sold, shipped back to Piber, or gelded and given other work. I saw these things happen, or heard about them, and did not think deeply about any of it, except to be glad that I continued in my own way to prove my worth and so was not dismissed. No, the careful culling of our ranks did not disturb me . . . until it happened, though under different circumstances, to Galant. To Ned.

It was a confusing time at *Die Spanische* . . . in the world, I suspect. We had been told that the German Army, the *Wehrmacht*, was taking over the school, as they had taken over Austria. The Germans brought a great uneasiness with them—a sense of uncertainty and fear that penetrated deep within the stone walls of our palace. Suddenly there were military men watching our exercises, roaming our halls, making inspections and (in our mind) a quite unnecessary bustle. From what I could gather, it seemed that now that Austria belonged to the Germans, so did everything in Austria . . . including a stable full of Lipizzaner stallions in the heart of Vienna. And the Germans were trying to decide what to do with us.

After a nervous day of army men striding about the barns and poking around our hay and halters, I was feeling quite upset, mostly because Max had been almost totally absent during their visit. I was pacing my stall, nickering for him, when Maestro admonished me to calm down.

"The Holy Roman Empire. The Hapsburgs. The First Republic. And now the German Reich. We have survived them all, and we will outlast this, too, Mercury. We are above the political machinations of the world," he said solemnly. I didn't have the heart to tell him that I didn't really care about the Germans per se, except when they were making a nuisance of themselves. It was Max I missed.

He was back the next day, even more subdued than usual, and he greeted me almost absently, though he spent a long time in my stall, brushing me over and over again, even when there wasn't a stray hair left to shed. He didn't put my tack on, or lead me out to the *Sommerreitschule*, or say much of anything. He just leaned against my shoulder, braiding and unbraiding my mane, checking nonexistent cracks in my hooves, then, finally, just petting me, silently.

We had more days like that—silent, thoughtful days—as

spring turned to summer, and Max's somber mood affected mine. Even worse, he had a few very uncharacteristic quarrels with the other élèves. In fairness, it was a stressful time for everyone (even without the Germans), so perhaps the spats were simply a release of tension. All three élèves—my Max, Ned's Georg, and Adrina's Stefan—were due for evaluations in the autumn, evaluations that could lead to their promotions to Assistant Riders. I remembered all too well what it was like to face the sort of inspection that could decide the course of your future. I was still a little amazed that I'd passed mine. Still, their voices were startling . . . so unusually cold and hot, rising and falling that morning, the first really hot day of the year. . . .

". . . don't see why you're making such a fuss about it. It's just a gesture!" Stefan sounded half-joking, half-angry as he led Adrina back to his stall after the weekend performance. Adrina and Ned had both been featured in the Young Stallions segment, and Max had helped demonstrate Maestro's magnificent levade in-hand. He hadn't wanted to ride at all, and had even told a fib that I seemed under the weather, but what with staff shortages and his own growing competence, he was always needed now. He was silent as he started untacking Maestro, his back to Stefan, who stood staring at him through the bars. Stefan apparently wasn't through.

"It makes us look bad–sloppy. Can you imagine how stupid you looked, just standing there with your hands to your side while everyone else graciously acknowledged the audience's applause? How ungrateful? How–"

"I don't care how stupid *or* ungrateful I looked, Stefan!" Max whirled around to face the boy in the corridor. "The only emperor I'm saluting in the *Winterreitschule* is Charles VI!"

"Who's that?" I nickered to Maestro.

He sighed heavily. "Holy Roman Emperor, King of Bohemia, Archduke of Austria. He had the *Winterreitschule* built. It's his portrait that hangs in the hall, that the riders salute."

"Ah. That red bit. Always wondered what that was."

Maestro looked too offended to respond, so he closed his eyes.

"Times change, Max! What's the big deal? Wait– stop. I'll *tell* you what the big deal is, actually. OK? It's that we were performing for some of the top officers of the *Wehrmacht*–men who very well might decide the future of *Die Spanische*–and you went out of your way to insult them!"

"Time is *not supposed to change here!*" Max practically shouted, jerking Maestro out of his snooze.

"What?" Stefan snorted. "What childishness—"

Max's voice crackled with emotion. "Every day we practice an art whose principles were set by Xenophon* more than two thousand years ago! *Die Spanische* itself was founded in the sixteenth century, for God's sake . . . look at the uniforms we wear, the traditions that are passed down from rider to rider. . . ." Max was growing hoarse.

"I don't need a history lesson, thank you very much," Stefan snapped. "I am much more concerned about the future. And if I were you, I'd be concerned, too. After all, the evaluations are coming up in autumn, and if the *Wehrmacht* is in charge of the school, I'm sure they will be looking very carefully into *all* of the riders' qualifications."

There must have been an undertone to this that I didn't understand, because the color left Max's face. I do believe he would have opened the stall door and hit Stefan if Georg hadn't intervened.

"Oh, enough, you two," he said cheerfully. "I admit

---

* Ancient Greek soldier and historian, author of the seminal work *On Horsemanship*

I think the salute's a bit silly. I think we should just take off our hats like we used to. Max has a point—we're horsemen, after all, not soldiers. Why should we be raising our arms in the air and shouting 'Heil Hitler'? But they want us to, so there you have it. Best to do what they say."

. . .

THINGS WERE SOUR BETWEEN MAX AND STEFAN after that exchange, though Georg tried to keep the peace. He wasn't always effective. Even a horse could see that Stefan had a decided opinion, Max had another equally decided but opposite opinion, and Georg really had no opinion at all, except that the arguments were a bore.

"Young Max is right, of course," Maestro told me as we walked to the *Sommerreitschule* for our morning lesson. "The fads of government have nothing to do with us. 'We are the makers of manners,' as the English poet said. At least, we should be. The world would be a much better place if people held its reins with a lighter hand."

I liked that—and liked that Maestro thought Max was in the right. Ned and I had reached no conclusions except that Stefan was becoming increasingly obnoxious. He'd always been a bit of a braggart, but friendly and dutiful. He took splendid care of Pluto Adrina and treated us all with affection. He used to be tolerant of Max's more quiet spirits, much as Ned had always tolerated mine. But no—that's not quite right. Ned had defended me, and I doubt Stefan would go that far for Max. At any rate, his mood changed with Max's, with the school's, with Vienna's. In the long, topsy-turvy days of summer, lines were being drawn.

And yet the figures we cut that summer and fall! I cannot think of that time without doing a mental pirouette, for the movement dominated my thoughts, despite all of our other work, from lead changes to improving my serpentines and renvers. But the pirouette, for a time, completely baffled me, so it looms large in memory. If my first and second years were all about going forward and straight, my third year was defined by learning to bend. At first, it seemed odd to me—after all, we'd taken all this time to address my crookedness, and now they appeared to *want* me to be crooked. Shoulders-in, or tail-to-the-wall, hindquarters swiveling, forelegs free, going forward but not *looking* forward, and trotting . . . oh, the trotting. It seemed all I did was trot. I am not passionate about speed, like Ned was back at Piber, but even I could have used a good canter up and down the length of the arena after a day of trot, trot, bend, twirl, trot, bend. But I don't complain of it. My body grew stronger and stronger, Max grew ever more secure and sensitive to my motion, and on days when I was really stuck, Polak would hop on my back and seem to perform the passade and renvers for me. He was positively uncanny, that man.

And then one day, it clicked. I had been thinking about the passade—essentially a small semicircle away from the wall, which I had been learning at the walk—and how I must try to limit the movement of my hind legs. Then it came to me. What if I kept my hind legs practically still altogether? Then I could turn a circle in place. Maybe Max would like that.

And he did. Very much indeed. Even Polak gave a bit of a whoop, which from him was quite something. I was stuffed with sugar and fussed over to an extraordinary degree. Apparently I had performed the pirouette very nicely, and even Maestro signaled his approval from across the hall, where he was displaying his piaffe. Now *that*, I thought, was what I wanted to master next. I loved watching Maestro, and while I did not harbor Ned's burning ambition for the Airs Above the Ground, I admit that I started to think that maybe, just maybe, there might be exercises I was good at, that I was . . .

even great at? Though I loved jumping things (streams, logs, my own shadow) in the natural world of the Piber fields, I suspected that I lacked the fire or dash to re-create the more dramatic movements, like the capriole, within the formal world of the school. I didn't have the confidence. Still, though I needed to chew it over with my hay, it might just be possible to loosen the borders of how I thought of myself, allow room for . . . pride?

"Will you look at that?" Polak said as he stroked my neck.

"What do you mean, sir?" asked Max from the saddle. They were really breaking all the rules today—whooping, talking, fluttering over me in a most maternal manner.

"Mercury actually looks pleased with himself! I swear he's practically preening!"

Max laughed and peered down at me. "He likes fig-uring things out. Yes, he does seem happy."

"Hopefully his mood is catching." Polak winked at Max as I nibbled on the tip of my rider's boot con-tentedly.

CHAPTER 8

MAESTRO CAME BACK TO THE BARN IN A very curious mood. I had just finished my hot walk with Fritz, the head groom (it was Saturday, a performance day, and I had demonstrated my pirouette in public for the first time), when the old stallion was clipped to the cross-ties for a sponging off after the School Quadrille, which is always the program's finale. His thick neck was arched as if he were still on parade, and if he were a cat, he would have had feathers peeping out from his mouth.

"Good ride, Maestro?" I asked. "You seem pleased with yourself, sir."

"No, not with myself, young stallion. I am pleased with someone else entirely. Granted, I am satisfied with the role I played in his performance, but it is mostly on the lad's behalf that I am, shall we say, cautiously optimistic."

Like many of Maestro's speeches, I had a hard time puzzling this one out.

"What lad?" It could have been horse or human. To Maestro, everyone except Polak and the senior riders were children.

"Oh, you'll see him later," Bonny called from around the bend of the narrow corridor, where he was being put back in his own stall after also performing in the quadrille. "Though he may look a little different!" Maestro wheezed a laugh, and his startled groom hastily withdrew the sponge, probably worried the cold water had brought on some sort of fit.

"Fine, keep me in the dark," I grumbled.

I wasn't left in suspense for very long.

. . .

IF IT WEREN'T FOR HIS FAMILIAR SMELL OF coffee and home (alas, not strudel, which he hadn't bought in months), I might not have recognized Max in his splendid new array. Gone was the élève's modest cap, replaced by one of Polak's winged headdresses! Gone was the dull gray coat; now Max was resplendent in a dark brown tailcoat with gold buttons and buckskin breeches. He seemed to have grown by a foot, and his eyes sparkled with a new expression of joyful pride that lifted my heart quite to the autumn sky. Max was no longer an élève. He was now an Assistant Rider of *Die Spanische*.

"There's still a pocket for sugar, Mercury," he said, and reached into his tailcoat to pull out a lump for me. The sugar was nice, but the happy look on Max's face, a look I hadn't seen in so long, was even better. I nickered my congratulations to him as best I could and tried to accustom myself to the way he looked in his new coat. Mine, to my chagrin, had still hardly changed. I was nearly seven years old and the most I'd achieved was a kind of dark, mottled gray, and a lightening of the ends of my mane and tail. Surely within the next year, I would become white; then Max and I would both look as we should.

"The uniform suits him, no?" Maestro accepted a sugar lump from Max, beaming fondly at the new Assistant Rider as if he were his own foal. If it weren't Maestro speaking, I would have suspected him of fishing for a compliment.

"Yes—but tell me how it happened! Sir."

"I was Young Max's performance partner, of course. Presenting a school stallion in the quadrille is the final test of the élève—and one he passed with flying colors. Of course, it didn't hurt that the horse he rode . . . well, that is to say, that his mount . . . ahem—"

I finished for him, so Maestro didn't tie himself into knots.

"That his horse was the most respected senior stallion in *Die Spanische*, a true teacher of men and horses. The *Maestro*," I said respectfully.

"Well, not that I would ever mention it myself, of course." The old stallion snorted.

I felt someone watching us and turned to see Stefan, Adrina's saddle piled in his arms. His face was red and sweaty, but it was the look in his eyes that made me draw back. His scent was acrid with stress, and his eyes were narrow and cold. He turned on his heel and stalked off in the direction of the tack room before Max noticed him. And he was still wearing a gray coat and cap.

. . .

THE DAY THAT MAX RECEIVED HIS WINGED HAT was the last truly happy day at *Die Spanische* for a very long time—I am glad that I didn't know it then, or I'm not sure I could have faced what lay ahead. War came. And it did what Maestro told me that all wars do—it wrecked. As I said at the very beginning of this tale, it did not change our world forever, but for several hard years, it consumed our lives and took from me all of the things I loved most.

The first thing it took was Ned. He had been chosen to participate in a tour of the horses and riders of the school to other towns—I do not know where exactly. He simply did not return. Bonny, who had also gone on the trip, told me that a high-ranking German officer had liked Ned's looks and "requisitioned" him for the cavalry. It was swift, and it was incomprehensible. I couldn't even say good-bye. One morning I came back from my lesson and there was a stranger in his stall—a young stallion just up from Piber, noisy and quarrelsome and self-announcing. My brother, my protector, my bulwark was gone.

But worse was to come. Everything happened so rapidly now; for a horse like me, who needs time to adjust to new realities, it was a series of body blows. I had hardly registered the *Anschluss** the year before, except when it affected Max's spirits (and brought the Germans to the stables with their everlasting inspections), but now the events of the world were no longer knocking at the door of the Stallburg: They were knocking it down.

"When's your train, Georg? I'm to report at the end of the week. On to Poland, don't you think?" Stefan's voice was exuberant, with a hard, triumphant edge.

"I'm going home to see my mother first," Georg

---

* The invasion of Austria by Nazi Germany in March 1938

replied. "My brothers are already enlisted—I'm the last. I can't believe my baby brother went up before me. They think I'm wasting my time, messing around horses. I'd rather mess around horses than mess around tanks."

"Maybe we'll serve together, eh? I'm applying for officers' school. But now that I'm in the Party, I've got my eye on the *Waffen-SS*. What about you?"

Georg stared at him. "You're in the Nazi Party, Stefan?" he said blankly.

Stefan laughed. He seemed in better humor than he'd been since losing out in his promotion.

"Maybe you didn't notice, but *Austria* is in the Nazi Party. Sure I joined—why not? It's the fastest way to promotion, and the Party's police force is the elite. If we have to serve, why not serve with the best?"

It took Georg a few minutes to answer, and his answer took the form of a question.

"And what about Max?"

"Well, Max wasn't called up, you know that. He has to go and register at the ICPC.* I was so surprised he

---

* The International Criminal Police Commission (ICPC) was a Vienna organization that started an international Gypsy registration in 1935. By 1940, the ICPC and its records were under control of the SS, an organ of the Nazi party.

hadn't already registered! His father hardly kept it a secret that Max's mother was a Gypsy. Everyone in the Austrian cavalry knew about the affair."

"His parents are dead," Georg said.

"Yes, what does that have to do with it? He's still half-Gypsy. He needs to register for his own safety. The SS must keep track of the Gypsies as well as the Jews. . . . it's wartime, after all!"

Georg opened his mouth to reply, then closed it again. He went back to brushing the stranger in Ned's stall.

. . .

THE COLONEL'S VOICE RANG DOWN THE CORridor, high and frantic with indignation.

"How in the name of Guérinière* am I supposed to form a cavalry detachment at the same time that I am attempting to preserve the art of classical equitation, take care of dozens of under-exercised horses, and do so with half of my staff conscripted by the army? Is this reasonable, I ask you? I may be more capable than most men, but this . . . *preposterous* situation is nearly beyond me! Now they tell me I must give up my newest Assistant

---

* The great eighteenth-century French riding master, whose training method forms one of the foundations of the Spanish Riding School's program.

Rider because he is, of all things, half-Gypsy! What, do they think he's going to steal the horses from under my nose? *Preposterous.*"

The man making this ruckus, directed at Fritz, our old, long-suffering head groom, was by now a familiar presence. Ned and Bonny and I had lumped him together with the Germans, since he showed up at roughly the same time they did and seemed to share their passion for inspecting and poking about. But eventually it became clear that this man, Colonel Alois Podhajsky of the Austrian cavalry, was more specifically in command of *Die Spanische.* Indeed, from listening to him, one might think it was his personal kingdom, and that the barbarians were at the door.

"I've got Nazi propaganda being printed in my staff rooms, renovations to the riding hall that will never be finished, and I owe back pay to nearly all my staff. At least they don't throw their arms up in that ridiculous salute anymore. The indignity! And I feel like hell. I am heading for a nervous collapse."

I believed him. In fact, many of us weren't feeling well. Illness came and went in the Stallburg—naturally with so many horses living closely together it was inevitable—but I had so far avoided getting sick. I was kept so well exercised, fed, and aired that it hardly seemed possible. I was a stallion in my prime—what business had I or Ned or Bonny or Adrina with ill health? But sickness and war go together . . . it's as if war were bent on stripping away all of my resources . . . first Ned, then health, then Max. It doesn't bear thinking about. I reeled from loss to loss, and I became very ill indeed.

The fever wracked my body for many months through that dark, cold winter. It was a constant, aching weakening of my limbs, and my breath came short and hard. All of the élèves and riders were gone, except for Max, and even Polak and the Colonel were nowhere to be found. The Stallburg was a silent, spiritless place, though Max and Fritz did their best to alleviate our discomfort and to cheer us up. They had their work cut out for them. Even Maestro grew ill, and in a stallion his age, that was worrying indeed.

And yet, I still had Max. That made all the difference in those long, feverish days. He had put away his fine brown uniform and adopted the simple garments of a groom, and worked with grim determination under the guidance of Fritz, as if he had never been promoted . . . had never been a rider at all. When the Germans were about, Fritz called Max "Hans," and treated him quite as an underling. I wonder where they thought the half-Gypsy Assistant Rider had gone? Luckily, the *Wehrmacht* officers seemed to have other things on their minds.

. . .

I SUPPOSE THERE WAS ONE MORE HAPPY LENGTH of days, though away from *Die Spanische* proper, and the memory is so bittersweet that it's hard to dwell on. After our sick, feverish, gloomy winter and spring, the Colonel came back—with a vengeance. He was indomitable, that man. He was so fed up with everything: the Germans, his ill health, our ill health, the deteriorating conditions in Vienna, his inability to get a decent cup of coffee, the lackluster uniforms, the poor quality of feed . . . the list went on and on and on, and we heard some part of his unending battle against the world every time he strode by us. He was like a noisy car—you hear it humming down the road (*grumble grumble army fools grumble*), a distant drone, then it gets louder and louder as it approaches (*grumble only person left in Europe who cares about the fate of man's greatest art . . . that hay looks moldy, grumble*), then roars by (*I WILL FIGHT TO MY LAST BREATH IF THEY CUT THE BUDGET THAT DRASTICALLY, GRUMBLE*).

The Colonel was determined to get us out of the Stallburg and into fresh air and a bit of freedom after our long, dull confinement. He was quite clear in his opinion of our looks—particularly mine—as he fed us tidbits and rumpled our forelocks.

"That horse started out looking like a weedy, unbalanced camel, and now he looks like a weedy, scrawny, orphan camel. Balanced, though. God, Max, do something to cheer him up!"

"He's always been a bit sensitive, sir," Max said. "The loss of his friend Galant hit him very hard."

The Colonel's face turned bright red and a vein pulsed at his temple. "Don't remind me," he barked. "Requisitioning a Lipizzaner for the *cavalry*. Preposterous."

"Yes, sir."

The Colonel lowered his voice conspiratorially. "How's it going, hiding in plain sight, lad? Can't last forever, I'm afraid, but we'll keep you as long as we can. Then to Switzerland, eh? Your father was a fine man, a fine officer. I was proud to serve with him."

"Yes, sir."

"And your mother's family?"

"The last message from my aunt said they were

being deported to some kind of detention facility, sir. Called Lety," Max said in a hollow voice.

It occurred to me then that one of war's primary functions seemed to be to *take* things. Ned, from being a star of the *campagne,* a handsome, gallant stallion with a future set by the dictates of his breed and its calling, had simply been taken. Gone. Max's family inexplicably was subject to the same force. It was like a mighty destructive wind was blowing through our world, and the Colonel, dear man, was standing in the middle of it, shouting his head off.

But he managed to find us fresh air. One beautiful morning in July, Max led me outside of the confines of the Hofburg for the first time in four years. As we walked through the tall wooden doors, I remembered our first stroll through the streets of Vienna, my sense of eager expectation, how brilliantly new and vivid the world had seemed. Now there was no Ned to follow, but at least I had Maestro, riding in style in a truck. There was a great uproar around the trucks—passersby had stopped and were loudly questioning the grooms: Where were they taking the horses? Was *Die Spanische* relocating to Berlin? How dare the Germans lay claim to Vienna's great treasure! The crowd was quite agitated, and it took

all the Colonel's soothing words to calm them down, which finally led to an invitation to follow the convoy to the Lainz Zoo*, our destination, which many did. I liked having the people walk with us–they reminded me of our honor guard of children on that first journey, years ago. I took my first steps onto the cobblestones and smelled coffee in the air. And felt Max's gentle hand on my neck. That was, yes, a good day.

---

* Not a zoo with wild animals, but a public parkland in Vienna

CHAPTER 9

THE LAINZ ZOO SEEMED LIKE PARADISE AFTER the grim winter. I regained strength in the bountiful parkland and in the large, airy wooden stalls that had been built just for us. To smell and taste grass again! A horse in his natural state will spend most of his time grazing—it's a sort of meditative nibbling that is the essence of peace. I hadn't grazed in four years, and I never thought I'd get enough of the sweet, tender blades of summer. It was a time of richness stolen from the very mouth of war.

We resumed our training under the warm July sun, but mostly each day felt like a vacation. And when Polak came back from wherever the Germans had been temporarily keeping him, it made our family nearly complete. Bonny and Adrina were positively exuberant, cavorting over the park like colts, and even Maestro looked young again as he ventured a prance around the tennis courts. I could not wander in this delicious freedom, over gentle hills and past thickets of dark woods, without thinking of Ned and our rambles in the mountains of Piber. I wondered where he was and what he was doing. I knew he was in the cavalry, and that meant fighting, but I could not picture it. I could only hope that if Maestro were right, and the Airs Above the Ground were military in origin, that Ned would finally master his longed-for capriole, and that it would sail him out of harm's way.

We managed most of our traditional exercises, enlivened (and distracted) by the open air and the occasional excitement of a wild boar running past the stables. Maestro admonished us to pay attention, to build back our strength, but the sunny fields were so different from the hushed solemnity of the *Winterreitschule* that I'm afraid we were a bit hard to manage at first. But horses infinitely prefer routine to novelty, so I was back to seriously working on my passage within a few days. Even better, one afternoon Maestro and I attempted part of a *pas de deux*, under Max and Polak, and though I bumped the old stallion a bit and was out of step for about half the time, it was great fun trying to match strides with the Maestro. We had to break up the exercise when Slava got away from his rider and tore across the tennis court to sink his teeth into Adrina's saddle blanket. The open air hadn't improved his temper, unfortunately.

"We hate that guy," I snorted to Maestro. He was too polite to agree, but he rolled his eyes in a marked manner.

.   .   .

MY LAST RIDES WITH MAX WERE UNLIKE ANY that had come before, and once I had conquered their strangeness, they were perhaps my favorite of all.

Instead of tight turns and subtle movements—progress by the inch, as our careful training went—we had acres of land on which to run. Run! I actually galloped with Max aboard, scaring deer and flushing birds from the grass! The Colonel had urged us to take advantage of the fields of Lainz, and we did—I leaped over brooks just as I did at Piber, but this time with a different friend running with me. Not Ned, but my Max, clinging gamely to the saddle as I used my body in ways I hadn't since I was a colt. As the smell of cypress and chestnut trees filled my nostrils and the damp earth cushioned my hooves, I marveled at what we could do together. Not only did Max teach me to dance, he also let my body sing. It was a piece of childhood, unearthed in us for a too-brief time, that I treasured forever.

The end of summer brought an end to our sojourn outside the palace. On a warm, star-strewn night, with an enormous August moon hanging fat and yellow in the trees, Max paid a late visit to our temporary barn, where Maestro and I were dozing in adjoining stalls. As I blinked sleep from my eyes, I was disappointed to see that the heaviness had returned to Max's shoulders. Like me, he had flourished in Lainz, turning nut brown and sort of relaxed and loose all over. But when he was melancholy, his whole form seemed weighed down— rather like a horse's does, actually. His eyes sparkled with tears in the moon's half-light, and as he fed me sugar, he buried his face in my mane. I stood very still, feeling him breathe against me. There is so little that a horse can do when we feel the sadness and anxiety of our companions. But we can bear their weight, so I held steady for Max as he cried against my shoulder.

"I will see you again, Schnecki," he told me. "And you, too, Maestro. I promise I'll try. There must be a place for us on the other side of this madness."

And I knew he was saying good-bye. I didn't know where he was going—if he was being claimed by the hungry war or if he was going on another path—but I knew in my heart that I would not see him in the morning. I neighed in distress, and he shushed me gently. When I wouldn't settle—and I couldn't, with the sour-feeling fear in my belly—he began to hum, and then to sing. I had never heard Max sing before, and the surprise of it was enough to stop my pacing.

> *All my dreams go back*
> *Where my sweet country is*
> *Green woods, flowery meadows*
> *And stands my old, old country home.*

> *I know I shall return*
> *Return, return*
> *My wanderings will end*
> *I'll be there again*
> *In my beautiful country.*

His voice was husky and cracked in places, but I loved the sound of it. It reminded me of birds at dusk, calling plaintively to their mates to come home, lamenting the end of the day and the setting of the sun. I wanted him to stay, to sing to me till the sun came up again, but he cupped my muzzle in his hands a final time, kissed me on my nose, and was gone.

THE COLONEL WANTED TO START PERFOR-
mances again, back at the *Winterreitschule*, but I had
little heart for them. I had little heart for anything, except for Polak, and since his promotion to *Reitmeister*,
head of all the riders, he was busier than ever. I tried
my best for him, but I was totally indifferent to the
German riders who had arrived at *Die Spanische* to build
up the depleted staff once more. I was stalled. Worse–I
was backsliding. I was getting nowhere with my passage, and soon I dreaded being led out of the Stallburg
to work, unless it was Polak's hand on my bridle. The
Colonel talked of sending me back to Lainz, or even to
Piber, but Polak was determined to try to bring me
round, step by belabored step. For him, I tried. Was
the horse still sick, the Colonel demanded? He had
shown such promise! I was sick–sick at heart.

"This can't continue, young stallion," Maestro said
abruptly one evening. "It is time to call upon your inner
resources."

"My what, sir?" I was in no mood for a lecture from
my imperturbable neighbor.

"Your *inner resources*. Your bloodline. Your abilities.
The things that serve as your bulwark in times of distress."

"But that was Ned." Hadn't Maestro noticed that I had lost all of the things that held me up?

"No—it is *not* Neapolitano Galanta. Nor is it Max Müller, or even Gottlieb Polak. Look within yourself. Do you remember being your mother's foal?"

Little did Maestro know that this was the worst thing he could have said.

"I was never my mother's foal," I said curtly.

Maestro looked at me curiously.

"She rejected me at birth. I was raised by Ned's mother." So there, I thought. Just try to jolly me out of *that* memory. I expected Maestro to be horrified. After all, no one in the Stallburg knew the shameful secret of my origins. Now I didn't care. Whose opinion was left that mattered, after all?

But Maestro, as ever, hardly twitched his tail. He looked totally indifferent to my shocking revelation.

"Ah, yes. She was probably too young to be a dam, or perhaps was sick herself. No matter. It wasn't your fault, and you soon found a proper mother. Now I understand why you and Ned were so close, of course. But as I was saying . . ."

It wasn't your fault.

"What do you mean?" I whinnied. "Of *course* it was my fault!" I felt completely overthrown.

"Hmm? Don't be ridiculous. Everyone knows that some mares aren't ready to be mothers at certain times, or circumstances prevent them from being so. It's not uncommon. Has absolutely nothing to do with the foal," Maestro said dismissively.

It wasn't your fault.

"You don't think that . . . there's something wrong with me? Sir? Like . . . everyone leaves eventually, and, well, there will never be anyone again who . . . loves me?" I felt ridiculous, but Maestro's words had unleashed a storm of feelings, and I couldn't bother to wait until I was coherent to question him.

"Do I think there's something wrong with you? No, except you're melancholic. Does everyone leave eventually? Yes—we all die. Is there anyone who loves you? I can think of many. Ned, who is still in the world, if not in the stall next door. Young Max, who is bravely fighting for his own threatened freedom. *Reitmeister* Polak, probably *Die Spanische*'s greatest teacher since Max von Weyrother,* who has taken a special interest in you, for which you should be honored. Your surrogate mother, who raised you so well that you became one of only

---

* Famed director of the riding school from 1813–1833

three horses to be selected for *Die Spanische* from your class at Piber. Colonel Podhajsky, who is so concerned about your health that he is thinking of putting you on a train back to the stud, which would involve considerable expense and inconvenience. The other horses in the Stallburg, from Conversano Bonadea to Maestoso Slava–whom you might notice never bullies *you* anymore–who think of you as "Uncle Mercury" and regularly comment that you're the smartest horse under saddle. And perhaps the feelings of your nearest neighbor, who has lectured you so frequently, are of no interest, but if they were then I might mention that you are quite dear to me as well. If all that isn't enough to live for, than I don't know what is."

I was stunned. It was all too much to fully grasp. I felt simultaneously guilt-stricken and possessed by hope.

"I'm . . . dear to you?" was all I could manage in response.

"Quite," Maestro snorted. "So pull yourself together, for heaven's sake."

. . .

MAESTRO COULD NOT HAVE TIMED HIS INTER-vention better, for that was the night of the first air raids over Vienna.

I could not sleep—I had too much to think of, and too much too feel, for rest—so I was already awake for the first wail of what we would soon learn was the air raid siren. Fritz was with us moments later, marshalling the grooms and directing our orderly procession from the Stallburg to the *Winterreitschule*. His hands were shaking but his voice was steady. The night air was cold and thick with noise and the first hints of smoke. I looked for stars but found the distant lights of planes. We passed quickly through the arches into the riding hall, where the Colonel, Polak, and the other riders were helping to secure other stallions, and pacing the length of the arena, looking to the windows, to the dark outside.

An air raid is really an incredible racket. From the waspish hum of approaching bombers to the thunderclaps of the bombs to the shrill tinkle of breaking glass—it's an orchestra of fury that reminded me of violent summer storms in the mountains of Piber. It's odd—we were nervous but not terrified, perhaps because we had all of the humans with us, perhaps because there was a bit of a festive feeling about being together in the *Winterreitschule* so late at night. One dependable school stallion thought we were here to work, and calmly executed a piaffe as we waited out the storm. Even Slava behaved himself. It was worse when the bombs came closer, shattering the windows above our heads and shaking the crystals of the one remaining chandelier that the Colonel hadn't taken down yet. Poor man, he felt the breaking of each pane of glass as a body blow, and he paced and swore and winced much more than we horses. But at the height of the attack, when even Maestro and I got a little jumpy, a new sound filled the hall and riveted our attention. It was, for us, the sound of our days, played at night in the midst of war, which was so strange, yet so sweet and fitting, that we stopped our nervous perambulations to listen with our whole hearts.

It was a song we often heard during our morning exercises, a song often played during our performances. The familiar, cadenced notes echoed up, up to the snowy, broken beauty of the hall around us, and despite the delicacy of the song, it was enough to silence the noise of the bombs around us. I looked for the source of the music—we usually had either a small orchestra or a gramophone accompanying our performances—and saw the outline of *Reitmeister* Polak, hatless, head bowed over the violin he played, his eyes closed, and his face nearly lost to the shadows cast by the flickering lanterns that were our only light. He played as the walls shook, and as the drone of the planes finally receded into the gray light of early dawn. I swayed in time to his bow; though he was only one man, with one violin, his music filled the school up to its brim. When the last note hung high in the great dome above us, it was succeeded not by explosions, but by the first birdsong of morning.

CHAPTER 10

THE HIGH WHISTLE OF THE TRAIN PIERCED the evening air, and Maestro and I turned our heads to it eagerly, more than ready to be on our way. We had had enough of air raids, enough of destruction, enough of the mad confusion of the past months. I was completely, thoroughly sick of the interruptions to my training, which in the wake of the loss of Max and my conversation with Maestro, I had thrown myself into with a fury, determined not to insult the memory of my friends or the good opinion of my neighbor and trainers. It hadn't been easy, what with the riders of varying skill that I bore, or with the occasional, baffling interruption to be hitched to carts to transport goods from one part of *Die Spanische* to another, but I was trying to stay on task. Maestro reminded me to do what I could, instead of wishing for what I could not have. But he also reminded me that it was permissible to hope, even in war.

And so I did hope. My hopes were not specific, but

rather centered around an idea of life for Ned and Max. Of course, selfishly, I imagined they could only be happy with me, as I could only be truly happy with them, but I was willing to picture them unhappy as long as I could imagine them alive and somewhat well. Amazing how war lowers one's expectations.

The train whistle blew again, scattering a few of the younger stallions like a flock of grouse, while the grooms scrambled to hold them together and in some kind of a line to board our boxcars. A thin blanket of snow covered the city, masking some of the scars of bombs, and lending an aura of late-winter peace to our walk backward from the Hofburg to the Südbahnhoff. We had mercifully been spared an air raid today, and now we were headed north, out of the path of the advancing lines of Russians and Americans who apparently had the upper hand in the war. We had lost most of our German grooms and riders to the front. Maestro said that he smelled the end approaching. I asked him what exactly "the end" smelled like, and he said, "Exhaustion, sweat, and homesickness." I suppose I could sympathize with that, if I had any sympathy for the Germans, but mostly I wanted them to go home, and to give back Ned and Max. The phrase "Don't let the barn door hit you on the way out" sprang to mind.

The Colonel was a man possessed. For months he had traveled hither and yon searching for a safe haven for his white horses as the armies converged around us. I believe he wouldn't have cared if wild boars suddenly entered the war and won it, so long as they left *Die Spanische* in peace and gave us our regular monthly allotment of oats. Now I watched him marching the length of track before us, inspecting our cars, checking feed, signing papers, and yelling at porters. It had been a tedious day of delays, and I suspected if we were held back much longer the Colonel might start brandishing his birch crop at the stationmaster.

We did finally board the train, and began our four-day journey north to the village of St. Martin-im-Innkreis. It was a long four days, relentlessly punctuated with warning sirens and all-clears. At times our cars were uncoupled from the engine and left on the tracks for hours, causing new paroxysms of fury in the Colonel. And at Linz, we endured a two-hour air raid, rattling in our boxcars like oats in a bucket, the Colonel and his wife tucked in with us. We bounced and winced and swore, but at least we were together. By the time we arrived at St. Martin, we were all so grateful for terra firma that we fairly leaped from the trains.

St. Martin was, appropriately, a castle, but like the

palace of *Die Spanische*, it was, in a way, under siege. The countryside was just beginning to soften into spring, and there was such peace in the rural scents of new grass and swelling waters that for a moment I could imagine I was back at Piber. The spell was broken by the conditions at the castle itself—a hive of men and animals who all looked like they'd really rather not be sharing the same quarters. Many of the men spoke in a strange, rough tongue and seemed ill and tired. Then there were clutches of Austrian women and children, equally unhappy and frightened, German soldiers with the smell that Maestro had pointed out to me, and at the head of them all, a Countess who was at once exasperated and bemused at what had become of her home. Refugee camp, POW camp, *Wehrmacht* headquarters, and now, home to sixty or so stir-crazy Lipizzaners.

I'm afraid we didn't make a very good first impression. They had built our stalls out of some absolutely delicious wood, and we happily chewed it all night long. I was delighted to see that after I nibbled away half my door, I could sidle out and visit Maestro. Bonny had discovered the same thing, and he joined us. Slava burst out of his stall and began terrorizing some of the younger horses, but we stayed snug at our end of the stable,

111

chewing bark and happily looking about us, until I shooed Slava away from the youngsters and sent him wandering out in the courtyard, neighing for mares. Adrina, unsurprisingly, joined him, and woke up half the castle. "Laaa-aaa-diiiieees! O Laaa-aaaa-diieeees!"

The Colonel was not amused.

· · ·

WE SPENT OUR DAYS HACKING IN THE countryside (and learning to seek shelter under stands of trees when we heard planes approaching) and watching the hurly-burly of what I would realize was the end of the war. We made friends with some of the rough-tongued men, and they occasionally helped with our grooming and feed, as we barely had a staff. And then one unforgettable afternoon, a new group of men entered our stable, bristling with weaponry, gray and helmeted and shouting as they opened our stall doors and poked through the hay: *"Hier nicht SS? Hier nicht SS?"**

"Ah," said Maestro. "The Americans have arrived."

"They have?" I asked, wondering who exactly "the Americans" were.

"Yes, young stallion. I believe our war may be over."

---

* "No SS here?"

We were taken from the stables so the Americans could turn them inside out, and as I stood tethered to a large linden tree in the courtyard, I watched the strange, fantastic scene. The last of *Die Spanische*'s German staff had hastily switched their military uniforms for other softer-looking clothes and stood about looking a little forlorn. Uniformed Germans had been crowded into a pen like so many cattle, if cattle were ever watched over by gum-chewing boys with guns. The Easterners (the rough-voiced men) were on some sort of a spree—grabbing armfuls of foodstuffs and lighting cigarettes with great satisfaction. The Colonel was talking to a man who looked from his bearing as if he were in charge of things now, and a gang of village children begged sweets from the soldiers. I was given a peppermint and a pat from one of the Americans and decided on the spot that they represented a change for the better. But it was what happened next that won me to them forever.

All day, American soldiers, Germans, villagers, and refugees streamed through the castle of St. Martin. They came on foot, by car, and by truck. I spent that sunny spring afternoon watching their procession, and was interested to see that one of the Americans—or so I guessed from the shape of his helmet, which looked like a basin

for water compared to the Germans' fancier headgear—
was riding a horse.

"Cowboy!" cried one of the children, pointing to him.

"Giddyup!" the soldier called back, grinning, and
spurred his mount forward. There was something familiar about the rattle of hooves on the gravel. I watched
curiously as they came closer, skirting the line of miserable Germans being added to the pen. The horse was
dirty, disheveled, and wearing unfamiliar gear. I strained
against my ties, hoping for a better view, raising my nostrils to the air to see if I could catch the stallion's scent.
And then he turned, stopped in his tracks, and sent a tremendous whinny over the courtyard:

"*Schnecki! Schnecki!* Are you here? *Schnecki!*"

With one leap, I snapped the rope that bound me to
the tree. I think I could have broken through any chains,
tore down any prison walls, or flown over armies and
battlefields. Joy nearly stopped my heart, but it gave my
feet wings. I suppose Mercury finally flew when the name
Schnecki was called.

The American wisely dismounted just before Ned
leaped forward to meet me, our trumpeting neighs echo-
ing off the ancient stone walls, bouncing off jeeps and
wagon carts. It was really Ned. Shaggy, thin, caked in

mud from his knees down, and looking happier than I'd ever seen him. The Colonel shouted for someone to catch us, Maestro and Bonny and Adrina set up a chorus of whistling, piercing welcome, and the American soldiers laughed, slapping their knees in childlike delight as Ned and I buried our noses in each other's manes and cried.

"Damnedest luck of all," someone was telling the Colonel as Polak held our bridles lightly, seeming to not want to interfere with us. "Captured this Jerry*–'scuse me, this German officer–who was keeping the horse at headquarters. Dick took a fancy to him, seeing as he grew up on a ranch, and we just kept him. Now we find you folks, in the very place he belongs. Look at those two! Always thought stallions just fought all the time."

"They are brothers," Polak said quietly.

I nibbled Ned's mane.

"I'm a P.O.W.!" he told me enthusiastically. "I was captured by an American soldier named Dick!"

"No," said Maestro, looking fondly at us in the last of the day's light, "I believe we are all finally free."

---

* A GI nickname for a German

EPILOGUE: THE NEW WORLD

A BRILLIANT WHITE LIGHT ILLUMINATED THE motionless horse, frozen in the ancient posture of cavalry statues, throwing the rest of the cavernous stadium into blackness. Over the loudspeaker a man's voice intoned, "The *levade*, performed by Favory Mercurio," and the strains of the accompanying orchestra were drowned out in a spontaneous eruption of applause. The horse's rider, a young Swiss who had been among the last trained by *Reitmeister* Gottlieb Polak before his death, was as still and calm as the horse beneath him, whom the éléves sometimes referred to affectionately as "the Maestro." To the horse, that title would never belong to anyone save the grand old stallion who had outlived Polak by only a few months. He liked to think that they were together, in some sunny pasture reserved for horses and the men who loved them.

Schnecki, as he still thought of himself, at eighteen years old was finally fully white-coated, though he

certainly remained the homeliest among his fellow Lipizzaners. But watching him perform the piaffe next to
the breathtaking stallions Neopolitano Galanta and
Conversano Bonadea (the star capriole artist) in the
quadrille that finished their performance, the spectators
did not think of his slightly odd looks—they marveled
at the seamless combination of power and grace, preci-
sion and strength, that were manifest in every movement
of the horses' bodies. But one man picked out the stallion, recognized his subtle, distinctive difference from
the other snowy white forms, and in his heart honored
him for everything that made him who he was: Schnecki, Mercury, Maestro. As the stallions lined up for a
final salute to the packed hall of Madison Square Garden, the man wiped the tears from his face with a hand-
kerchief, replaced his gray hat, and smiled down at the
young child sitting beside him.

"Let's go meet some old friends," he told her. The girl
did not hear. Her eyes followed the horses from the
arena, and her heart was filled with hoofbeats.

· · ·

IN THE FIVE YEARS SINCE THE END OF THE
Second World War, the white Lipizzaners of Vienna
had yet to set hoof back in their rightful home. They

had instead become citizens of the world, touring Switzerland, Italy, and Germany, and, when not on the road,
lived in ancient Dragoon barracks in the country. By
the time Favory Mercurio sniffed the salt tang of Bre-
men, hoisted high in the air in a strange crate to the
deck of an enormous ship, he had seen enough of the
oftentimes inexplicable world to feel at home in it, even
when swaying like a gull in the ocean breeze. Now he
had braved a squally, four-week passage to the city of
New York and had witnessed the overpowering can-
yons of buildings, their dark shadows swallowing whole
streets, while up, up in the sky their windows shone in
the brilliant autumn sunshine. The dock swarmed with
men in hats with cameras, shouting, "Smile! Look happy!
Smile!"

"In America," said the Colonel, as if trying to explain
to the riders what this all meant, "everything is of course
gigantic."

. . .

THE MAN STEERED THE SMALL GIRL THROUGH
the crowd, saying, "Pardon me" as he craned his neck for
a better look forward. He smiled at the mixture of people
who had been drawn to the horse show—men in formal
eveningwear, women in long dresses, but then a large

assortment of women with children in everyday clothes. *In Europe,* he thought, *horsemanship is a man's world. In America, it is for the women and especially the children.* It was a happy thought, and he squeezed the shoulder of the girl beside him.

There was a large clutch of eager bystanders pressing against the velvet rope partitioning the audience from the backstage area of the Garden. The man picked his daughter up and swung her onto his broad shoulders so she could catch a glimpse of the white horses being untacked, groomed, and fed treats. He reached into his pocket and pulled out a half a strudel, the best he could find in the Brooklyn bakeries, and handed it to the girl.

"Let's see if we can give the horses a treat, Lydia," he said. He pushed his way forward as politely as possible, but then as he caught sight of a familiar head, Roman-nosed, intelligent eyes sparkling with life, his manners deserted him.

"Mercury!" the man cried out.

The horse threw his head back, ears pricked, nostrils flared. His eyes darted rapidly over the crowd, then looked on all sides of his enclosure and even behind him. He whistled through his nose, and let out a tremendous whinny that sent reverberating *ooh*s and *ahh*s through the crowd.

And then another man was shouldering his way through, from the other side of the velvet ropes, ignoring the hands reaching out for his, the pens stretched forward for his autograph, the eager clamor of the ladies calling, "Colonel! Colonel!" And Alois Podhajsky drew Max Müller's arm through his own and led him forward through the crowd.

The ladies and gentlemen and children who saw the tall, thin man embrace the noble stallion, and saw the tiny, fair-haired child offer him a treat, did not know who they were or how many miles and years it had taken to reunite them, but they knew love when they saw it— they knew tenderness when they saw it—and they knew through their own war what it was to find the person you loved again after the world had taken them from you. And so they burst into applause.

AUTHOR'S NOTE

WHILE MY PREVIOUS BOOKS IN THE BREYER Horse Collection involved forays into, for me, unknown territory and history—twice to the American West, and a brief trip to the coal mines of Scotland—*Mercury's Flight* took me further afield both in time and place . . . and required quite a lot of help to get right.

My first thanks must be to Atjan Hop, former secretary general of the Lipizzan International Foundation (www.lipizzaninternationalfederation.eu.com) and founder of Baroque Consult (www.lipizzan.nl). Atjan is not only an authority on the noble Lipizzaner breed, its training, and its history, but was also the kindest, most thorough, and most generous of readers, saving me from numerous errors and cheering me on throughout two drafts.

I would not have met Atjan had it not been for Andreas Hausberger, head rider of the Spanish Riding School in Vienna, who kindly allowed me to join

the Horses and Dressage Web site and listserv (http://
horsesanddressage.multiply.com), which he manages. This
deeply knowledgeable and vibrant community gave me
expert guidance on everything from how horses got from
the train station to the Stallburg in 1930s Vienna, to
Gottlieb Polak's violin; from training techniques to stall
bedding. In addition to Andreas, who answered many ques-
tions himself, I must particularly mention John N.
D'Addamio (who gladly learned, and gladly taught).

At the Spanish Riding School, I am indebted to Barbara Niederberger-Sommersacher, who helped me with
the depiction of the inspection process at Piber, as well
as created a general timeline for a stallion's progress
through training. Die Spanische has a beautiful Web
site (www.srs.at), as does the Federal Stud Piber (www.
piber.com).

I was ridiculously lucky to have the translator
Krishna Winston's help in coming up with the perfect
Viennese nickname for my thoughtful, slow-paced stal-
lion: *Schnecki* (little snail).

And it is lucky for students and aficionados of the
Lipizzaner breed that its most valiant protector, Colonel
Alois Podhajsky, was a prolific writer with a firm sense
of his own place in history. These books of his were

123

essential to the writing of mine: *The Complete Training of Horse and Rider in the Principles of Classical Horsemanship* (reprinted by the Wilshire Book Company), *My Dancing White Horses: The Autobiography of Alois Podhajsky* (1965, Henry Holt), and *Die Spanische Hofreitschule* (1954, Verlag Adolf Holzhausens NFG).

Of course, none of these marvelous sources could save me from willful error for the sake of narrative. While I made every attempt to get as factually and historically correct as possible, there were times in which I felt I had to take liberties with facts for the sake of fiction. First, the new recruits from Piber would never have been allowed to run freely in the *Winterreitschule* with older, territorial stallions—they would have been by themselves. Second, I've condensed some of the events of the war years into a shorter space of time. And last, Gottlieb Polak died before the evacuation of the riding school—but I couldn't bear to lose him. His violin solo during the air raid is, alas, a fantasy. While I rather doubt there were any half-Gypsy élèves at the school during the war, there is no doubt at all about the persecution of the Gypsies in Austria before and after the Anschluss.

Lastly, heartfelt thanks to Miriam Altshuler, Susan Bishansky, and Jean Feiwel for their patience and trust.

ANNIE WEDEKIND grew up riding horses in Louisville, Kentucky. Since then, she's been in the saddle in every place she's lived, from Rhode Island to New Orleans, South Africa to New York. Her first novel, *A Horse of Her Own*, was praised by *Kirkus Reviews* as "possibly the most honest horse book since *National Velvet*. . . . A champion." She lives with her family in Brooklyn, New York. www.anniewedekind.com